RUBY CELESTE
AND THE GHOST ARMADA

RUBY CELESTE
AND THE GHOST ARMADA

Nicholas J. Ambrose

RUBY CELESTE AND THE GHOST ARMADA

Nicholas J. Ambrose
Copyright © 2013
All Rights Reserved.

REGARDING THE HIVE

Discover more about Nicholas J. Ambrose,
the Ruby Celeste universe,
and more at
Regarding THE HIVE
http://www.regardingthehive.co.uk

Drawn and quartered,
this book is dedicated to
Emma,
Alex,
Gem,
and my mum,
for helping me through.

I am so thankful for all of you.

Lars Drury Makes a Call
(Prologue)

1

The trill of a telephone cut through the afternoon. It rang once, twice, and then on the third chime a hand plucked it from its cradle, taking care not to smear neon green nail polish on the plastic.

Tucking the phone between ear and shoulder, the woman resumed coating her fingernails and answered, "Rhod Stein's office, *The Pharmacologist's Eden*. How may I help you?"

"Hi, Charlotte. It's Lars, from Equity." He sounded tired, Charlotte thought—though that could well have been the cost-cutting connection. "Is Rhod around?"

Swiping a green stripe up one nail, Charlotte dropped the brush carefully, so that it wouldn't ooze on the desk, and fanned her hands. "Can I take a message?"

"Afraid not; I need to speak with him pretty urgently."

Charlotte glanced at the great wooden doors leading into Rhod's office. Closed, imperial, menacing. She lowered her voice. "Are you sure? You know how he is."

"Believe me, I wouldn't be speaking with him unless I absolutely had to."

"Okay, I'll put you through. Two seconds."

2

Another phone rang: the one perched on Rhod's expansive desk. Swivelling in his chair, the hulk-like director swung around and picked it up in fingers like sausages.

"Yes?" Even alone the word was somehow threatening; not an inquiry but a demand for information; information that must be delivered *quickly* and *concisely*.

"Mr Stein, I have Lars Drury on the phone for you," Charlotte said.

"Who?"

"Lars Drury, sir. From Equity. He says it's important."

Leaning back in his seat, Rhod reached into a drawer and withdrew a fat cigar. He rolled it idly between his fingers. "Put him through."

"Yes, sir."

The phone went momentarily dead. Then it chirped back into life with a half-second tone, preceding a brassy background noise that pervaded most of the lines here.

Rhod waited.

Two seconds went by, and then a voice spoke, sounding rather more nervous than when it had conversed with Charlotte. "Good afternoon, Mr Stein." A noise like a clearing of the throat, followed by: "This is Lars Drury, from—"

"I know where you're calling from," Rhod cut across. Placing the phone on the desk, he keyed it onto speaker mode. Without bothering to stifle the rustle of plastic, he unwrapped his cigar and said, "What is it?"

"I have a customer here interested in the purchase of Property 23. He, ah—he said you personally verified the sale."

"And?"

"We already accepted an offer on Property 23 yesterday. From one ..." Papers rustled in the pause. "Ruby Celeste, of the Pantheon. She's due to arrive in two days' time."

Rhod took a lighter from his breast pocket. Gold glinted along its edges. "Well, I'm overriding the sale."

"Sir? I don't …"

"Listen," Rhod said. "The fellow you're dealing with now offered *three times* Celeste's buying price. *So*, I'm overriding the sale." He bit off the end of the cigar, spat the stub out, and lit up. "Make sense?"

Rhod could picture Drury now: his mouth flapping. A satisfied sneer on his face, he swivelled the chair around to stare through the enormous window that made up the rear of his office, and down at the kingdom—the *empire*—he had built.

"Sir, what about Miss Celeste?"

"Her sale still proceeds."

"But—"

"I'll take care of it."

"Sir—"

Rhod turned back toward the phone. "Make the sale," he barked. "I've got this." And before Lars could say anything else, he jabbed a thumb down on the hook and terminated the call, then replaced the receiver in its cradle.

Lifting himself from his seat and puffing smoke, Rhod wandered to the window. It went almost from floor to ceiling, and wall to wall: a clear two metres in height, and another six wide. And beyond, below, he watched with a smile as his SkyPort bustled: *The Pharmacologist's Eden*, a cubic mile of shops and vendors and patrons, hung perfectly in the sky.

He took the cigar from his lips and rolled it in his fingers, a thin plume of smoke snaking a dirty line in the air.

Yes, he thought. Property 23 would be sold, and then replaced—and Celeste would never know.

The Pharmacologist's Eden
(Chapter One)

1

A knock sounded at the office door.

The young woman looked up from below her tricorne hat and brushed a crimson curl out of her face. "Come in."

It swung open, and in stepped a rather tall, somewhat gangly fellow. He was decked out in a long, thick brown overcoat, and under one arm was perched a clipboard. Though it didn't show from here, a bald spot was just beginning to form toward the rear of his head, forming a ghostly hole in his greying black hair.

"We're almost there, Miss Celeste."

Ruby beamed. "Excellent!" She pushed her papers to one side, rose, and strode across the room. "Well, off we go."

In the corridor, the two fell into step. Ruby, though shorter, was faster, and it was only at a brisk pace that this man—her assistant—kept up.

"How far out are we?" Ruby asked.

"Miss Brady estimates a mile and a half."

Ruby nodded. "Good." She gave the man a sideways glance, and her lips twitched. "Oh, do look pleased, Trove. Just think: we're gaining more than just a new deckhand today. The pantry will be restocked."

"Ah, yes," said Trove. "New meals for Mr Wyler to molest and obfuscate. I do so look forward to it."

Ruby gave a tiny shake of her head, smile still on her lips. "Samuel's cooking is perfectly satisfactory."

Trove smirked. "If you insist."

The exit to the deck loomed ahead: not a staircase but a metal ladder poking up through an opened porthole. Ruby took the rungs and hoisted, careful of the skirts bunched around her legs. Halfway up, she glanced back.

"Smile, Trove."

He fixed her with a put-upon look. "Get up on deck, Captain, or you'll miss the view."

Ruby shook her head, but there was a glint of teeth as she resumed climbing. "See you topside."

Up the last few rungs and then she was on deck, beneath brilliant mid-morning sun raging down from perfectly clear skies.

The Pantheon was part of the SkyHugger class of ships—a strange combination of rustic and techy. Eighty metres from rear to prow and twenty-seven wide, she was an angular, boat-like thing. Externally the hull was wood, but this was only show: it was bonded to a rigid steel shell which housed three inner levels. Apertures pocked the exterior; three cannons on each side plus a large one running from front to back, along with several cameras.

Sprouting from the topside deck were three great fins. Enormous notched triangles, the front and rear were over thirty metres tall, while the central fin towered to almost fifty metres in height. Intricate patterns crisscrossed their surface, a subtle reddish gleam muted by the daylight.

Right now the deck was empty; downstairs, all hands were working to ensure the next few hours went smoothly. Mostly that meant tidying and organising the contents of the Pantheon's rather empty bowels, ready to be restocked.

At the front of the deck, Ruby stood, resting her hands on the metal rail that snaked the Pantheon.

Up ahead floated *The Pharmacologist's Eden*. Even from here Ruby could see the SkyPort's size; a handful of ships were manoeuvring around it, smears compared to the hulk that was the *Eden*.

"Impressed?"

Ruby glanced rightward, to Trove, who looked forward with his hands folded behind his back.

"Suitably," she answered.

"I hear it's one of the largest for several hundred miles."

"I believe so." Ruby watched as it grew imperceptibly nearer, widening by mere millimetres with each passing second. "It's rather pretty, compared to some of the others."

Trove made an indifferent noise, and Ruby suppressed a grin. "Smile," she reminded. "Today will be fun."

An eyebrow rose on Trove's face. "Dodging hordes of shoppers? I cannot wait."

Ruby tutted, but stopped herself from punching him in the arm, instead tracking the ever-nearing *Eden*.

2

The SkyPort comprised two distinct sections. The upper part of the *Eden*, home to open plazas and storefronts, took the top two-thirds of the structure. The other third beneath 'ground level' held the parking bay, which wrapped around the entire port, and inside that a fortress of metal and piping that housed the many systems, automated and not, that kept the SkyPort running.

Approaching the parking bay was a brief logistic firestorm, and Ruby retreated into the Pantheon to oversee the process from the ship's control centre. It involved lots of stopping and starting and constant radio contact with the *Eden*'s technicians—but after ten minutes they managed to pull into a vacant bay.

"Ship is officially docked, Miss Celeste," Natasha Brady— navigation leader—announced. "We're free to board."

A palpable sigh of relief went up. Docking with SkyPorts was never usually this complex; others *always* had free bays, so it involved simply drawing close and stopping. None of the juggling and constant communication of this place.

"Okay, folks. Let's board," said Ruby. "Once we're at ground level, we'll amass and discuss." Turning to Trove, she said, "If you could inform the others."

"Already begun, Captain."

A metal walkway, sans railing, had extended alongside the Pantheon. For all its treacherousness, the crew sauntered along with nary a glance nor twinge. At the end hovered a young man in a blue and black uniform, who greeted them all brightly as they passed. His eyes flicked momentarily to the scabbard at Ruby's waist; she gave him a nod, passed, and then waited a short distance away for Trove. The wait was brief; the last few stragglers made their way off the ship, before Trove crossed the walkway rather rigidly.

"You look uncomfortable," Ruby remarked as they fell into step.

"I was expecting a rail."

"Hah. No Benjamin?"

"You sound surprised."

"I thought he might be able to tear himself away for at least an *hour* or two."

Trove laughed. "No such luck. You know Ben."

Ruby shook her head. "I suppose I ought to have known. He is rather …"

"Obsessed?"

"*Studious,*" Ruby finished.

"What's to study?" Trove asked as they reached a set of metal stairs leading up to *The Pharmacologist's Eden*'s ground level. "It's a great round thing that eats and lets us fly."

"It's more to him."

"I tell you what I think it is."

Ruby cast a sidelong glance at her assistant. He waggled his eyebrows suggestively, and it took everything Ruby had not to snicker—and even then, *something* escaped her lips. "Oh, be quiet, Trove. Come on, let's get on. We've got work to do."

3

The Pharmacologist's Eden was immense. In the middle, ground level was wide open, filled with markets and stalls, as well as fountains and miniature parks. Stacks of stores formed a horseshoe around three of the *Eden*'s sides, towering at least a dozen storeys skyward. Chrome edges glinted in all directions.

The crew of the Pantheon were already gathered beside a large fountain as Ruby and Trove stepped up.

"Afternoon," Ruby said.

A rabble of responses, just as jovial as Ruby to set foot off the ship for the first time in over two months.

"Should I assume we all know what we're doing?" Ruby asked.

"I should bloody well hope so," said a male voice. "After three days of prep." A round of titters went up around him.

"You will thank me, Mikhail," Ruby said, "when you've finished restocking the ship in an hour and have another two with which to amuse yourself however you so please."

Mikhail stuck out his tongue; Ruby reciprocated, before going on more seriously, "I expect this to be smooth. From what I hear, Mr Stein runs this place tightly. *However*, if anything does go amiss, you know how to get in touch."

Murmurs agreed. At least one person's hand twitched up to his opposite wrist, and the thin electronic bracelet strapped beneath his sleeve.

"Well, I shan't keep you. Be off, and enjoy the next few hours!"

A cheer went up from the Pantheon's crew, and in moments the cluster had dispatched into twos and threes, all heading off in different directions; some toward maps, others following signs, and those most eager, who had memorised the layout already, to their destination.

Only Ruby and Trove remained behind.

"Shall we be off?" Ruby said. And without awaiting a response, she began to move, and Trove hurried behind to keep pace.

4

The Pharmacologist's Eden was everything Trove had feared: gaggles of shoppers, moving in uneven throngs that the curly-haired captain navigated with ease, but which Trove always seemed in danger of crashing into at a moment's notice.

"None of the others are like this," he huffed after narrowly missing a pair of men wrestling some exotic, leather-skinned beast toward the parking bay.

"None of the others are this *large*," Ruby said. "And besides," she added, "very few have a marketplace specifically for willing deckhands. That's why we came."

"Perhaps we should have gone without."

"And run with marginally less efficiency?" Ruby asked in mock disgust. "No, Trove, that simply will not do."

The place they were going was a little outfit called Equity. Unlike the majority of vendors here, who rented a storefront on the *Eden*, Equity was owned and run by the head honcho himself, Rhod Stein. Not that Ruby expected to deal with the man; if the radio conversation was anything to go by, he was entirely detached—except, of course, for his pockets. With a place this large, that fact was unmissable.

They soon arrived. A wide open archway led into the place, all sleek and shiny, the store's name emblazoned across the arch's top. Beyond was a small desk, manned by a single diminutive fellow, and then white walls into which doorless entryways were sliced.

Ruby strode to the desk. "Good morning." Her eyes flicked to the man's nametag: LARS DRURY.

Lars looked up from a ream of paperwork. His eyes darted from Ruby to Trove. When he opened his mouth to speak, his lips twitched.

"Good morning," he said. "Do you have an appointment?"

"We do indeed. Ruby Celeste, of the Pantheon. We spoke several days ago regarding Property 23."

"Ah." Lars licked his lips, and his eyes dropped to the papers, just for a moment. "Yes, well, right this way, Miss Celeste."

Stepping out from behind the desk, he led Ruby and Trove through the nearest opening.

The white walls were not walls, it turned out, but dividers: eight feet tall, and arranged in a maze of right-angles. Ruby glanced into a few as they passed, but each was as empty and nondescript as the last. Clinical and showy, with sparse decoration; a lone shelf with two books and a creeping plant.

They made their way into a 'room' toward Equity's rear. Lars glanced from Ruby to Trove and back again. Licking his lips again, he said, "I shall be right out, Miss Celeste. One moment, please." And without another word, he disappeared through the gap in the wall.

Ruby started counting. When she reached ten, she muttered, "Something's not right."

"I beg your pardon?"

"Something's not right," she repeated. "He's edgy."

"Perhaps his day is not going as expected."

Ruby didn't respond. She didn't believe that for a moment, and by the twinge in Trove's voice, she doubted he believed it either.

Besides, even if she wanted to, she couldn't have said a word, because no less than a full second later there came a clatter from somewhere close by, followed by raised voices.

Trove tensed. Ruby mentally checked her scabbard, overcoming the urge to reach for her sword's hilt.

The scuffle became louder, closer, and as it did Ruby began to pick out words from the frenetic mess: asking for … release? She shot Trove another sideways look and mouthed, "What the—?"

Something crashed into one of the dividers forming this makeshift room. Trove leapt; Ruby's hand flew to her sword, ready to draw.

"Let go of me!" shouted a man.

A deeper, gravelly voice: "Easy, kid."

The divider shuddered again, a couple of feet closer to the

entryway. Ruby's eyes narrowed.

Lars stepped back through. Still his eyes darted, more to the floor now, and the Pantheon's captain noticed his ears had turned scarlet.

Drury was followed by two of the thickest, tallest men Ruby had seen in her life—and between them, miniscule in comparison, was clutched a thrashing black-haired man.

"This is Property 23," Lars muttered.

"I'm *what*?" the man shrieked. "What the fuck is—"

A fat elbow smashed the side of his head, and his last word was turned into a grunt.

"What the hell is going on here?" Ruby demanded.

"Property 23," said Lars. He refused to meet the captain's gaze. "This is the deckhand you're here to purchase."

"It most certainly is not," Ruby scoffed.

"Deckhand? I'm being *sold*?"

"*Quiet*," one of the man's captives growled.

The black-haired man's eyes went wide, fixed to Ruby's. More whites than brown, they screamed two things: confusion, and fear.

"I can assure you," Lars began, but Ruby cut him off.

"You can assure me nothing. I was told that I would be purchasing a *deckhand*, six feet tall, weighing two-twenty-five. This guy is barely taller than me, and looks like he weighs all of one-fifty soaking wet. This is *not* the deckhand I was promised."

The purported deckhand opened his mouth to say something else, but the heavyset man to his left twisted his wrist, converting it into a whimper.

"You've lied to me, Mr Drury," Ruby said, her voice rising.

From somewhere behind, Trove said, "Miss Celeste …"

"Or was this all set up by Stein?" She stepped forward—another step, she realised. "Is he that much of a pompous, tight-fisted *asshole* that he thinks I'd commit the oversight he's surely praying for?"

Trove, again: "Miss Celeste, I really think …"

She was just inches from Lars. Her right hand, the one she'd rested on her sword's hilt during this whole conversation, lifted, and she moved to jab the man in the chest. "Do you *really* think I'm *that stupid*?"

"Miss Celeste!"

Two things happened very, very fast. The man who had stood to the fake deckhand's right had broken away and inched across the space just as Ruby had, and just as Ruby's finger made contact with Drury's chest, the man swung.

At the same moment, Ruby ducked.

The swing went high, almost toppling the man off-balance—and then Ruby was up, sword drawn.

Someone cried out—the deckhand?—and in her periphery Ruby saw Lars scrabble from the room.

The guard threw a ham-sized fist at Ruby. She danced back a step, and swung her sword. A splash of red arced up and the man howled; he reared back, left hand slammed to the inside of his elbow, where claret gushed between his fingers. His right hand hung dead by his side.

There was no time to savour the victory; the second guard had already broken away from Property 23 with a sideways swipe and marched forward. "*Get out!*" he roared, swinging his fist overhand to smash the top of Ruby's head.

She dodged, and the fist whistled through air. As it passed through the space her shoulders had resided a second ago, she swung her sword again, this time low. The blade sliced fabric, skin and then muscle with barely any resistance, tearing a crimson streak through the man's left side. It was so fast, so smooth, that the blade had already cleared his body before the blood began to flow.

Down he went.

"Quit screaming," Ruby said. "You sound like a little girl."

"I'll kill you!" the first man yelled. He had fallen against the wall. Blood smeared the white behind him and was pooling beneath his limp arm. "I will *kill you*!"

Ruby cast him a momentary glance, but no more. He was out.

She gave her blade a cursory flick to rid it of blood, then sheathed it.

Her eyes scoured the room. Lars had vanished, but Trove was safe—had barely moved, in fact, though he looked rather pale—and the kid they'd tried to fob her off with was still here, askew upon the floor.

Ruby crouched beside him. "Get up."

He stared. There was even more white to his eyes now. "W-what?"

"Get up. We're breaking you out." Then, more to herself, she muttered, "No one tries to scam Ruby Celeste.

"Trove, recall the crew," she said, returning to her feet.

"Right away."

"You won't get away with this!"

"Oh, be quiet," Ruby muttered with a backward glance. "You're rather distracting, and you ought to be concentrating on holding what little blood you have left in." Addressing the black-haired man again, she said, "It's imperative you move. We need to be out of here."

"I—" he started, but no more came from his lips.

"Come on." Ruby extended a hand, took the man and pulled him in one fluid movement to his feet. "Are you hurt?"

He was breathing hard, she realised, and white. A whimper escaped his lips, and he clamped his roving eyes tight.

"What?"

"I don't like blood." The words came out strangled and forced.

"Well, we'd better get moving then." Casting a backward look at Trove, who nodded from above the wrist-bound communicator he was speaking into, Ruby said, "Let's go." And, after clamping a hand tightly around the man's arm, they were off.

5

It was almost impossible to control his wildly shaking fingers, but Lars somehow managed, from one of Equity's back rooms—

because there was *no way* he planned on calling from the front of the store and encountering Celeste on her inevitable departure—to dial the number to Rhod's office.

"Pick up, pick up, pick up," he whispered desperately as the phone trilled in his ear.

Finally: "Rhod Stein's office, *The Pharmacologist's Eden.* How may I help you?"

"Charlotte! It's Lars. I need to speak with Rhod."

"Can I take a message?"

Lars scrunched up his eyes, clasped a hand to his forehead. It came back damp with cold sweat. "No, Charlotte, I need to speak with him."

"Um … Rhod said he didn't want to be interrupted by any calls—"

"*Charlotte!*" Lars shouted. "I need to speak with him *now*. Tell him Celeste just pulled a sword on the two members of security he dispatched this morning!"

There was a brief, terrifying pause, and for an awful moment Lars thought Charlotte might try to redirect him again—but then she said, "I'll put you through."

6

From behind her desk, Charlotte eyed the great wooden doors to Rhod's office. He had been irate at first, but once she'd passed on what Lars had told her, he had silenced. Now the two were talking, and Charlotte wondered exactly how long it would be until— what? She wasn't sure, but uneasiness bubbled in her stomach as the seconds lengthened.

She didn't have long to wait. The doors burst open and out marched Rhod, seething rage written on his face. Charlotte jerked in shock, moved to greet him, but he was already past, barking orders into a radio—and was that a *gun* in his other hand?

He pushed through the doors at the end of the room and was gone, leaving a wake of silence behind.

Charlotte waited. Her breath held in her chest. *Something* was happening on the *Eden* today, something involving Lars and a man or woman called Celeste.

Lars!

Heart rate rising, she grabbed the phone and called Equity.

It rang, and rang, and rang.

No one answered.

Lowering the phone back into the cradle, Charlotte stared off into space. Her mind seemed both frozen and a chaotic mess all at once.

Then she pushed out of her chair and headed for the doors Rhod had just passed through.

7

Rhod hit the stairs and hurtled down them two at a time.

Things had gone wrong today. Kidnapping the kid had been a mistake; a willing deckhand should've been shuffled into the empty hole left by the original Property 23. It was too late now to fix the error—but Rhod could stop this chain of dominos before the cascade got too far.

What would Celeste do, he wondered? Rhod didn't think she'd remain at Equity; no, he had a feeling she'd do all the damage she could, and then depart. With the kid? Possibly. *Probably.* She would want to get *something* out of this excursion.

Which meant right now Celeste had to be heading back to her ship.

Rounding a corner and moving down the next flight of stairs, Rhod lifted the radio affixed to his belt and called down to the parking bay. An attendant answered a moment later; Rhod cut him off before he could speak. "This is Rhod Stein. There's a ship called the Pantheon down there now, owned by Ruby Celeste. I want to know where it is."

"Yes, sir. Please bear with me as I consult our records."

"Got it?"

"Not just—here we go. Bay 16A."

Rhod thumbed the radio off, then placed a second call.

"Security—"

"Dispatch to parking bay 16A."

"Sir, half the available workforce are on their way to Equity—"

"Then dispatch the *other half*," Rhod barked, and hung up.

At the bottom of the squared spiral of stairs, he pushed through glass double doors and out onto *The Pharmacologist's Eden*'s bustling ground level. Somewhere out there, returning to her ship, was Celeste—and Rhod was going to find her before she left this place behind.

8

"The crew are returning to the ship as we speak," Trove informed Ruby as they passed out of Equity.

"I trust you told them to make haste," said Ruby.

"I certainly did."

"Good. Drury was missing; calling additional forces, no doubt. We may be apprehended in the parking bay." The captain licked her lips, eyes scouring the crowds. It was busier out here now; midday looming, the clientele was nearing its peak. "Or sooner."

They wove through the heaving throngs, Ruby leading with one hand clamped firmly around her captive's upper arm. His breaths came in gasps, and Ruby was acutely aware of how they looked, dragging this man at a march.

"I need you to look natural," she muttered.

"What?" the man breathed.

"They'll have sent security out after us, and I'm willing to bet more than the two I just took on in there." The man clamoured, but Ruby ignored it. "We'll look like prime suspects unless you act more natural."

"I—I don't—"

Ruby froze. Her captive's momentum kept him moving for just

an instant, and he stumbled into Ruby's field of view before being jerked back.

Trove, who had become separated once again, hurried up. "What is it?"

Ruby's eyes tracked the position of the men she'd just seen as they moved through the crowd. "Security; a pair. Eleven o'clock … ten."

The man moaned again.

Trove searched. He was a head taller than Ruby, but all he saw were faces, dozens and dozens of them, moving in every direction.

"Shouldn't we move?"

Ruby nodded. "This way." She pivoted twenty degrees off their original path and resumed walking.

A minute later Trove jogged up again, one hand plastered to his hair, and panted, "I think we lost them."

A sigh of relief went up from the man at Ruby's side, but nothing happened to decrease her tension. It would take security just moments to realise she had left Equity—and stolen the alleged Property 23. After that all security would converge at the parking bay. And given all the theatrics involved in docking with *The Pharmacologist's Eden*, they would know the exact ship they were looking for.

She shook the thought from her head. That was an issue for later.

"What's your name?"

The black-haired man gaped at her. "What?"

"What's your name?" she repeated.

"Oh—um, Francis. Francis Paige."

Certainly a better moniker than Property 23.

"I'm Ruby Celeste."

She gave him a sidelong glance, just for an instant, before focussing on the people surrounding her again. He was still pale, still licked with a sheen of sweat, but his footing had improved. The fresh air had to be doing him good.

"Are you going to take me home?" he asked.

One of Ruby's eyebrows twitched. "Let's just focus on getting you out of here alive for now."

9

Hurrying down the stairs to the parking bay, Ruby's eyes scanned the row ahead. A crowd had gathered around one of the docks, and Ruby had a fairly good idea even before she hurried up whose ship it had congregated outside.

Voices muddled over one another, all pressing for most volume. As Ruby got close, she began to pick out snippets; most her crew, others not.

"What's the meaning of this?"

"If you'll just please calm down—"

"Calm? Where's Captain Celeste?"

Ruby pushed into the crowd, and the voices hushed almost instantly. She sidestepped several members of her workforce, dragging Francis behind her, and then found herself at the front of the group, facing a foursome of attendants who blocked the gangway to the Pantheon.

"What's the meaning of this?" she demanded.

"We're under instruction not to let anyone board this ship," one of the attendants replied. He sounded confident, even in spite of the dozen men and women facing him.

"Oh, really?" Ruby countered. "Who's going to stop me?"

"Security will be here in just a moment; they'll—"

Ruby drew her sword in one fast, fluid movement. Stepping forward, one hand still wrapped around Francis's upper arm, she pressed the blade to the side of the attendant's neck.

Eyes blazing, through gritted teeth Ruby muttered, "Let me on my damn ship *now*."

10

Two bleeps: the radio. Snatching it up, Rhod opened the channel. "What?"

"Mr Stein, sir, this is the parking bay." It was a man, and his voice was panicked. "We've had a problem, sir."

"*Spit it out.*"

"Miss Celeste arrived; she drew a sword on us, sir."

So that was her game. Well, Rhod thought as he rearranged the gun in his right fist, he would put a stop to that. She wouldn't even get a *chance* to swing that blade of hers.

"And you held your ground?"

"We *did*—"

"God damn it!" Rhod shouted. The roar echoed above the bustle, and more than a handful of alarmed faces looked in his direction.

"Sir, we were outnumbered—"

"*Don't let her leave,*" Rhod barked, before clicking the radio off.

He took a mental check. Still over a third of the *Eden* to cross before he arrived at the parking bay.

Damn it!

He gripped tighter on his pistol, slapped the radio back into its place on his belt, and broke into a run.

11

"Everyone, on the ship," Ruby said.

The crew didn't need telling twice; they hustled past and up the gangway double-time. Ruby did a headcount; fourteen, herself included. Even with Benjamin already on-board, there were still two members of the Pantheon's crew somewhere on *The Pharmacologist's Eden*.

Natasha Brady held back as others passed. She snapped to attention. "Instructions, Miss Celeste?"

"None yet, but get to the control centre and I'll meet you in a few moments. We're still waiting on two," Ruby said.

Brady snapped off a salute. "Aye." She cast Francis—who was moaning quite unabashedly—a funny look, and then hurried up the gangway.

"Any instructions for me?" Trove asked. Only he, Ruby and Francis remained now.

"Who's left on the *Eden*?"

Trove rolled up his jacket sleeve and consulted the computer at his wrist. Ruby waited, eyeing the attendants huddled a dozen metres or so away. They were speaking animatedly, and one had been talking on the radio a few moments ago. Calling security? Stein? One of the two, without question. Ruby's time was rapidly running out.

"Evans and Peters," Trove said. "They should be with us—ah."

Two men hurried along the parking bay—empty-handed, a distant part of Ruby noted.

One of the attendants moved to step forward, but Ruby held up a hand and fixed him with a fiery glare, and he backed away.

"Sorry," Evans panted, clutching his side.

"No matter; just get on board," Ruby said.

They abided.

Ruby glanced at Trove and nodded. "After you."

He gave a brief nod of his own and scurried up the gangway. Ruby moved after him—and met resistance.

She turned. Francis stood stock still, his eyes closed firmly. His breathing was quick and ragged again.

"What is it?" she hissed.

"It's—there's no rail."

Another twitch of Ruby's eyebrow. "We need to get out of here," she said. "And the only way to do that is this way."

"I—what if I fall?"

"Then I'll *catch you*."

"I don't want—"

There was no more time; down the same staircase she, Francis and Trove had come less than two minutes ago came a full *pack* of men: thick-chested, bald-headed, all in white, and all carrying guns.

Ruby gritted her teeth. "You don't have a choice," she said to Francis—and then yanked him by the arm and up the gangway as fast as her legs would carry her.

"Stop!" someone yelled—more than one person, actually—but Ruby paid no heed. Dragging as hard as she could on the man behind her, her only focus was up ahead: the entryway in the Pantheon's railing, and then its porthole.

A pistol-like crack snapped the air in two—no, not pistol-like: it *was* a pistol, Ruby thought as, at almost the same instant, sparks flew from the railing a metre ahead. They had opened fire!

"Oh God!" Francis yelled.

"Just move!"

More gunshots; two bullets were lost to the open air, while the third threw up a tiny explosion of wood from the Pantheon's deck. The fourth hit the rail right where Ruby passed, and she pressed her body lower, aware that it wouldn't matter either way.

"*Stop! Thief!*"

They reached the gap in the railing. Ruby spun, pushed Francis forward onto the deck first. He looked petrified, and no wonder: there were at least a dozen men hurtling along the parking bay, taking pot shots. A few precious seconds and they would reach the gangway.

"Come on!" Ruby ran across the deck, Francis a half-step behind, to the open porthole. "Get down there."

"But—"

"Now!"

He didn't need telling twice.

Another pockmark exploded in the decking barely a foot ahead of Ruby. She threw her arms up against the spray.

Francis was down the porthole. That was good. Everyone was on-board. Also good.

Another crack whipped through the air, and something hot

burned Ruby's neck. She grunted and slapped a hand to it.

"It's been swell," she muttered, then lowered herself onto the ladder. "But it's time to go."

Wood exploded into fragments around her, and sparks flew from the porthole hatch—and then she was down and pulled it closed.

Francis cowered against one of the walls, and beyond waited Trove. Paige's eyes flicked to Ruby's neck, and he closed them and winced. His breathing was laboured, worse than it had been inside Equity.

"Are you—" Trove began, but Ruby cut across.

"I need you to find a place to stow Francis until we're safely out of here."

Trove nodded.

"Will you be okay?" Ruby asked the captive. Her voice softened just fractionally.

Francis gave a tight little nod.

"You're in safe hands." To Trove, Ruby said, "I'll be in the control centre when you're done." And up the corridor she strode, leaving the two men behind, heading for the Pantheon's beating heart.

12

The room was heaving when Ruby stepped in; every station was manned, all anxiously awaiting Ruby's orders. The plethora of screens were lit with camera feeds directed at *The Pharmacologist's Eden*.

Natasha Brady crossed to Ruby as she entered. She snapped off a salute.

"At ease."

Brady relaxed. "You're bleeding."

Ruby ignored it. She stepped past the navigation leader and to the main console, peering at the largest display of all. Currently it showed the *Eden*'s parking bay, which was sinking as the

Pantheon rose.

"Direct thrust away from the SkyPort," Brady instructed her team, but Ruby held up a hand.

"No. Just lift the ship for now."

No murmur of confusion came, but Ruby felt the air change in the room. Brady stepped forward, hovered at her captain's elbow. "Miss Celeste?"

"Raise the ship." Ruby looked back at Natasha, then at the console once more. She pressed a hand to her neck, to the place the bullet had grazed, and withdrew it. Maroon smeared her fingertips. She glanced at it with distaste. "No sense leaving without a parting gift."

13

A hundred metres—ninety—eighty—

Rhod was almost at the stairs to the parking bay. Would have been already were it not for all these *fucking people*! But he was almost there, and that Celeste woman would have what was coming to her, and he would relish doing what his sorry excuse for a security team couldn't—

He juddered to a halt. Three great notched sails had lifted above the ground level. That was nothing unusual, as ships came and went all the time. But they continued to rise, and now a ship lifted into view, moving higher and higher, staring down the *Eden*.

Right at the front was an aperture, wide open, and extended from within was a halo of steel, glinting in the midday sun.

For one terrifying second, Rhod knew exactly what was about to happen. He knew what ship this was and who captained it. And in that moment he knew the sheer scale of the error he had made.

Then there was a blinding flash of light and the world exploded.

Francis Paige

(Chapter Two)

1

"I warn you, Miss Celeste, this may sting."

Ruby sat in the Pantheon's medical bay, laid back and skewed to one side on a thin plastic bed. Darrel Stitt, the ship's aging doctor, was perched by her head, rubbing a tiny needle in a cloth doused in alcohol, followed by the surgical thread that hung from it.

"Go ahead."

"Always brave, Miss Celeste." The doctor placed his rag aside and pushed the needle through skin. A low hiss escaped Ruby's mouth. "Though you'd do well not to get shot next time."

"It was a grazing blow."

"Then you'd do well not to take a grazing blow."

The room itself was not far from the control centre, placed at the rear of the Pantheon's middle deck. It doubled as office, operating theatre, and ward all in one: a wide semi-circle that spanned the ship from side to side, it was a separated by foldable dividers that extended up and down the floor in little troughs. Unlike the majority of the ship, which was filled with dark wood and antiquated decorations (save the lower deck, the cafeteria and the kitchen, of course), this one was all plastic: green and what had once been white, but was now somewhat yellowed.

As Darrel stitched, Ruby cast her eyes up to Trove, who stood patiently by the bed, eyes averted.

"You look as though you've never seen blood before."

"It's not the blood that causes discomfort," Trove countered. "More the needle and thread moving in and out of your neck."

Ruby pulled a wan smirk. "Your report, Trove?"

"I have questioned the crew. We acquired … rather fewer resources than we set out to."

Damn it, Ruby thought. But she had known, of course; they had been on the *Eden* for less than twenty minutes, and fully restocking the ship took a good hour at best, even with all hands put to work.

"What did we come away with?"

Trove consulted his clipboard. "We have food to last us the next week, but it'll be tight; we were already down to the dregs upon arrival. Mikhail and his team succeeded in returning with a sack of pellets for the Volum, but no munitions, though he advises our armoury was still half-stocked upon arrival."

Ruby gave a tiny nod, which made the pull on her neck worse. She winced, and Darrel tutted and rearranged her head with his free hand before continuing to stitch.

"One set of first aid materials, a single set of filters for the water condensing units …" Trove's eyes sailed down the meagre list. "And that's it."

"Nothing for maintenance?" Ruby asked. "Oil for the cannons?"

"Those were on Mikhail's to-do list."

Damn it. Almost everything was running low except for the stuff they *didn't* particularly need, and with seventeen mouths to feed—no, eighteen, Ruby reminded herself—they needed to at least stock the ship's pantry as soon as possible.

"How close is the nearest SkyPort?" she asked.

"You mean aside from the one you just put a hole in? *Wainsbridge* is closest; at full speed we could make it in four days, but it's behind *The Pharmacologist's Eden*; we'd need to pass it again, or at the very least draw a wide loop, extending the journey to six or seven days."

"Any others?"

"*The Oft-Trodden Footpath*; that one is five days away."

Ruby nodded. Darrel huffed.

"I suppose that's where we're headed then," she said.

"Miss Brady anticipated that; we're on the way as we speak."

Ruby mulled over their state of affairs. Food was definitely the priority. They could watch out for passing flocks of birds, perhaps toss out the nets to grab at those that came too close—but even that would only extend their pantry levels minutely. No, it was clear: they had to move to the next SkyPort with as much haste as the Volum could muster.

Not, she supposed, that it would mind.

"There we go," Darrel finally said, snipping the thread protruding from Ruby's neck. "All buttoned up." He retrieved a clean cloth, doused it in rubbing alcohol again, and pressed it gently to the wound; it burned a dull ache and Ruby's eyebrow twitched. "It might bleed a little over the next couple of days, so I would advise taking it easy."

"You know me," Ruby said. "Careful."

"Hah, yes. Let me just apply some gauze to catch the flow."

Protective pad taped down, Ruby was at last free to leave the doctor, and Trove able to look at her once more—though he did wait until they were safely from the room, the door closed behind them.

"What now?" he asked.

"Take me to Francis," Ruby said. "I have a few questions to ask."

2

Francis had been stowed in one of the empty crew quarters on the Pantheon's first level. The door was locked from the outside, and Trove reached into his jacket for the key. He went to insert it into the lock, but Ruby held up a hand.

"We have manners, Trove," she said. "We knock."

She rapped twice, then permitted Trove to proceed. She opened the door and the two stepped inside.

If Francis had looked lost before, he looked worse now. Though the room was not particularly large—one bed, a wardrobe, a desk and a small amount of open floor space—he seemed minute, sunken onto the bed and leaned against the rear wall. His knees were bunched together and held in his arms.

He looked up, slowly. There was still fear on his face; less, but there.

"I have some questions for you," Ruby said carefully.

Francis glanced between the two. "Are you taking me home?"

Ruby licked her lips. That was twice now he'd asked that. "Where is 'home'?"

"Down there."

Ruby frowned. "Down where?"

Another glance from Ruby to Trove and back again. And then Francis answered; two words alone.

"The surface."

3

Tension pulled the atmosphere taut. Ruby looked sideways at Trove. His expression was exactly the same as she felt: perplexed.

"What do you mean?" Ruby asked. "You mean—*down there*. The surface. The *ground*." She groped desperately for something to say, something Francis hadn't already told her. "You're not from up here?"

He shook his head. "No. But—but you can take me home, right? You saved me from that—that place—and you can take me home, can't you?"

Ruby hesitated. So much fear—but that sheen of hope lighting his features!

And yet, she couldn't lie.

She spoke, slow, careful, her voice measured. "We can't."

"... w-what?"

"I'm afraid we can't do that. *I* can't do that. The Pantheon ... this ship is designed to fly. It has to stay airborne. If it dips too low, it won't lift again. It's just too heavy."

Francis's face sank. Then something seemed to click in his mind, because the hopeful look came back. "But those people came down and took me. They—they could do it. You could take me to someone who can take me home."

Ruby shook her head.

Francis's face dropped. "Why?"

Ruby sighed. She sat down at the foot of the bed. "It's expensive. Most people don't have the tech. The only person within a few hundred miles that could—well, I just tore his SkyPort in half."

Silence. The last light slipped from Francis's face.

"So there's nothing?" he finally said.

"Not that I can do. But you can stay here," Ruby added, trying to sound at least a little upbeat. "This room here, it's yours now. We're like a family. Trove can show you around the ship, and—"

She stopped. Francis had drawn his legs into his chest as far as they would go. Face hidden, his shoulders shook. No sound; his sobs were masked.

Ruby stood. Her heart broke for this man: abducted, taken away from everything he had ever known. She wished she could do something, anything—but there was no way. Not now.

Quietly, she crossed the room to Trove. "Let's leave him to his thoughts."

They stepped outside, and Trove pulled the door closed softly behind them before joining Ruby at her elbow.

"That took an unexpected turn," he said.

Ruby was quiet. She reeled, searching for holes in her thoughts, ways she might somehow be able to take Francis home. There were none.

"Come on," she said at last. "I'd like to check the extent of the damage to the deck."

Ablaze

(Chapter Three)

1

Flames roared, staining the sky with a towering streak of black smoke. It would be hours before all the fires were put out; long past nightfall, maybe even beyond dawn, Rhod guessed as he staggered through the ruined *Eden*.

Celeste's attack had been devastating. The rear wall of storefronts had been targeted dead centre –right where Rhod's office once was. The blast, at such close range, had torn down two-thirds of the wall. The remainder had been distorted by the impact; at the edges several levels had twisted or collapsed, great beams contorted at terrifying angles before terminating abruptly.

Fire teams had been dispatched, and the *Eden's* water reserves were being pumped as hard as they could go while the SkyPort's crew attempted to combat the flames. The condensers were being pushed to the absolute limit to draw as much moisture from the sky as they could to quell the inferno.

People had died. Rhod couldn't even comprehend the sheer number that had to have been vaporised in the blast: hundreds, at least. More were surely trapped under the rubble, asphyxiating as their lungs filled with smog.

There had been a mad dash for the parking bay as almost every person on the *Eden* fled. Even some of the staff had tried to escape; Rhod had seen their stricken faces as they passed in the chaos, thought of reaching out and grabbing them—but then he too was bustled and tossed about, and they were gone. Now the only people here were the staff that hadn't abandoned the port and the few survivors desperately searching for lost souls.

Now he hobbled across the ground level, away from the wreckage. Away from the screaming people, pawing desperately through warped metal and concrete. Away from the dozens of hoses aimed at the blaze. Someone reached out as he passed, wailed something incomprehensible, but Rhod shrugged the woman off, his face dazed, eyes vacant.

He trekked across the ground level; past smaller, localised fires. Rubble had ricocheted in this direction, great chunks, taking out entire stalls, fountains, devastating half of a miniature public garden. A cluster of bodies lay slumped in formation, heads and shoulders missing, and beyond that a great steel rod that had ploughed through a railing before coming to a halt.

He walked and walked. Passing the middle of the *Eden* the rubble was less and less; only the smaller pieces carried this far. Facing forward, the sky was blue: no fires burned here.

Step by step, Rhod's mind began to move again. Cogs turned. He would have to repair the *Eden*. It would be costly. There would be some kind of insurance to pay, without question; measures to prevent this happening in the future.

But before all of that, there was something more important: Celeste.

2

"It just happened so fast," Lars said. Leaning against Equity's façade, one arm draped over Charlotte, who clung to him, his eyes stared straight ahead, taking in nothing. "She pulled the sword, and then ..."

"I'm so glad you got out okay," Charlotte whispered. Her eyes were pink, though her tears had subsided long ago.

The Pantheon's attack had come barely moments after Charlotte reached Equity. Her focus on getting to Lars had been so single-minded she hadn't even seen the ship. One second there was the

Eden's usual hubbub; the next a deafening boom, then nothing but screams.

"If you hadn't come," Lars began, but his words died. There was no need to finish. They'd both seen the destruction, the vacuum where the office had once been. Where *Charlotte* had once been.

They were still, quiet.

Lars jerked to his feet. Charlotte spluttered as she was tossed aside. She shot him a look, but followed his eyes and gave a little gasp before hurrying up herself.

Rhod Stein approached.

"Sir," Lars began.

"I want to use the phone."

That was all he said before he was past.

Lars watched him disappear. Charlotte stood beside awkwardly. She bit her lip.

"Should we follow?"

Lars shook his head. "I'd rather not."

"We should go," Charlotte muttered.

Lars hesitated a moment, then took her hand. "Okay. But only over there. Just in case."

They wandered away to wait.

3

Rhod strode through Equity, around the maze of dividers. A pool of maroon seeped around an edge, and he saw in the corner of his eye a thick-bodied man slumped sideways against the makeshift wall.

Rhod didn't pause.

The rear end of Equity had two doors: one to the small quarters that housed the men and women waiting to be sold, and one to the diminutive staff office. It was this second door that Rhod shoved through.

This room was nothing compared to Equity's front end. No

white, no decor. Instead it was brown, lit by a single stained bulb that cast more murk than light. A couple of rusted filing cabinets were shoved against one wall, their drawers stuffed, and beside another was a cheap desk with a computer and telephone. A swivel chair was placed in front of the PC; its wheels were missing.

Rhod hefted down into the seat and picked up the phone.

Most of the phones across *The Pharmacologist's Eden* were designed for one purpose: dialling the rest of the port. They could place calls to other locations on the hulking construction, but none outbound.

Or that was, at least, what the staff were told.

Rhod counted to five, then keyed in eight digits. He paused, and a moment later the tone pulsed, just once. That was what he wanted.

He dialled and waited.

"Hello?" someone answered. The voice was female, and scratchy even over the tinny sound of the line.

"It's Rhod Stein."

"Ah," she said, drawing the noise out. "It's been a while."

"I have a job for you."

"I'm listening."

"A woman called Ruby Celeste just stole a deckhand from me, then blew a hole in my SkyPort."

"And you want me to get the deckhand back?"

"No, Imelda," Rhod growled. "I want you to hunt her ship down and kill her."

There was a pause. Rhod knew the drill: she was weighing it up, determining a cost. Trying to make him squirm.

At last Imelda said, "It may be dangerous."

"Price is irrelevant."

"Aha." There was a touch of glee to Imelda's voice. "Well then. You'll have to send the details. Picture of the ship; presumably you have one. Its last known whereabouts." She snickered.

"I'll forward data shortly."

"*Good.*" She drew out the word again, lengthening two 'O's to five. "And you want me to kill her."

"That's right," Rhod answered.

"The proof?"

"Her head."

"Mm. And the deckhand?"

Rhod pressed his lips together. "Irrelevant. I want Celeste's head on a stick. The rest—ship, crew, the deckhand she stole— torch it."

The Pantheon

(Chapter Four)

1

Francis had had next to no sleep, drifting off only in the early hours when his body finally gave out on his mind. The dreams he had were brief and fevered, and now swam away as low knocking awoke him.

The bed was a bedraggled mess. He had slept in his clothes, and they too were askew.

God, he hated this place already.

That same knocking came again, followed by a voice: "Mr Paige?" It was the man that had brought him here in the first place, the man that accompanied the captain—Ruby, her name was.

"Mr Paige, it's Trove."

Francis was tempted to roll over and simply go back to sleep, to shut the man out. After all, Trove would give up sometime, wouldn't he? Report back to Ruby that his attempts had been unsuccessful.

But again he knocked, and Francis knew he couldn't ignore him. Pushing out of bed, he traipsed across the small floor and pulled the door open, glaring at Trove through tired eyes.

"Ah, good morning. I wasn't sure if you were awake."

"You woke me." Francis looked at Trove sourly. "What do you want?"

"Miss Celeste has requested I take you on a tour of the ship."

Francis looked up and down the empty corridor. "Too important to do it herself?" he grumbled.

"Miss Celeste is rather tied up at the moment. Duty calls a captain." Trove stepped aside. "Should we begin?"

Francis gave a last look back at the room. But there was nothing for him here: no change of clothes, no activities he might busy himself with, and no excuses.

"I guess so," he said, resigned, and stepped from the room with an inward sigh.

2

"This ship is called the Pantheon," said Trove. "It's split into three decks, not including topside. The one we're on now is our residential deck; mostly it's comprised of crew quarters, much like your own, a communal area and a library. I imagine most of your time will be spent here, while you, err, adjust."

Adjust. He was stuck, Francis thought for the hundredth time. Kidnapped, then kidnapped again, and now trapped on this floating ship for—how long? The rest of his life? Until the reckless woman that captained this thing got them killed by pissing off someone even bigger than she was?

"And here is the ladder topside. Would you like to go up?"

Francis shook his head. "No." Even thinking about the fact they were floating miles above ground made his stomach lurch. "Thanks."

The residential deck was much the same throughout. Wooden, with long crimson carpets. Paintings were hung here and there. Each door had a small brass plaque, a name and number stencilled on—or, in the case of one door Francis eyed as they passed, a pair of names.

The library wasn't much larger than Francis's room; maybe bigger by half, it wasn't much of a *library*: only two bookcases stood in here, and their shelves weren't quite full. Two plush chairs were parked around a battered coffee table, while a great wooden globe perched in the corner.

The communal area was somewhat larger, but still rather

vacuous. There were some chairs, and as Francis wandered through the seating without interest, he noticed they were all bolted down.

"The next deck down is more like the Pantheon's heart," Trove said as they took the stairs between levels. "Our control centre is here, along with the medical bay, the canteen and kitchens, and a number of smaller operations rooms. It's here that we have navigation and cannon control."

"Cannons," Francis repeated in a hollow voice.

"We have one long cannon facing fore and aft; it runs the full length of the ship," Trove explained. "There are also several smaller cannons to each side. Rest assured, if the ship is attacked, we're well-defended."

Attacked. Well, that didn't make Francis feel much better.

Francis stopped, and Trove halted beside him. He turned and waited.

Francis placed a hand against the wall of the corridor.

"This place is made of wood," he said at last.

"Sort of," Trove said. "The exterior and interior are, but it's all bonded to a steel hull several inches thick. If we take a blast, the damage is mostly aesthetic."

Francis gaped. "Mostly."

"I shan't lie; there have been a few close calls in the past. But Miss Celeste knows what she's doing."

Yes, Francis thought. Of course she did. She'd only had the two of them almost killed yesterday. Getting shot at—getting shot herself, even—was clearly the mark of someone who was in control.

"Besides, holes in the hull can be bonded closed again," Trove said, continuing up the corridor. "It's nothing we're not used to."

"How does this thing stay up?" asked Francis. "It's made of steel. It's got to weigh …" His mind boggled as he tried to pick a number, before finally finishing weakly, "Tonnes."

"Aha. Good question. Come with me and I'll show you."

3

The lowest deck was nowhere near as fancy as the others: the walls and floor were solid steel. For the most part it was a storage level, split into several sections: a pantry for the kitchen, a sizeable munitions room, and a general storage bay full of maintenance equipment. The only real room was located toward the rear, and took up a full half of the level's floor space.

"This," Trove said as he knocked at the door, "is what keeps us up."

The door opened to reveal a rather annoyed-looking man who stood midway in height between Francis and Trove. He was middle-aged, his brown hair awry, creases lining his clothes. Several days' growth of facial hair adorned his thin cheeks.

He cast Francis barely more than a glance before fixing upon Trove. "Yes?"

"This is Francis Paige," said Trove. "We, err, acquired him yesterday during our brief stay at the *Eden*."

The brown-haired man looked at Francis again, for longer this time, before returning to Trove. "Okay. And?"

"I'm giving him a tour of the ship, and thought he might like to see the Volum."

"I'd rather not—"

"Come on, Benjamin. It's at Miss Celeste's request."

For an instant Benjamin looked like he might fight, but he relented and stepped inside. Trove crossed the threshold into the room, and Francis hesitantly followed. As he passed, Benjamin instructed, "Don't touch anything."

The room they found themselves in was … well, Francis didn't know how to describe it. It felt more like a cavern. Tabletops and shelving were set up madcap about its perimeter, stacked full of ledgers, and on the nearest table there were at least five books, all open and filled with blue scrawl. Two fat sacks of dark pellets were shoved in a space; one had tipped over and spilled its contents across the floor.

But the strangest thing had to be what was in the centre: a vast, globular thing with leathery skin. It seemed to breathe in and out slowly, and emitted a blue glow around the room that pulsed in perfect cadence with its breaths. There was a small face that looked desperately out of proportion, but even that was simple: a pair of eyes, closed in clear contentment, and a lipless mouth that hung open.

From the top of the creature sprouted dozens of wires that crisscrossed the ceiling before disappearing into holes toward the upper decks.

"It's sleeping, so don't disturb it," Benjamin warned.

"Yes, yes," Trove said. Turning to Francis, he said, "This is the Volum. It keeps the ship aloft."

Francis stared. This deck was twice as tall as the others, and now he saw why: to house this thing.

"What *is* it?"

"Its sole purpose is to eat; those high-energy pellets over there, specifically. As a by-product of its eating, it generates lift, as well as a sizeable … 'pocket', shall we say, of calm."

Francis frowned.

"It negates wind," Trove clarified. "Wind speeds up here would be catastrophic; this thing quells them around the ship quite nicely." He paused. "Well, most of the time."

Francis lifted an eyebrow. "What are those wires?" he asked, pointing.

"They link up to the fins on top of the ship, as well as the control centre and our batteries. In nature a Volum's lift is omni-directional; there's very little control over it. But our ship's fins take a portion of that lift and point it in a single direction, allowing us full navigational control. It's rather useful, I'd say."

Mouth agape, Francis listened. This was incredible; like nothing he'd ever seen. Slowly, eyes scouring the creature, he walked its circumference. Benjamin made a noise, but Trove waved him down and he stifled.

"It glows," Francis said simply.

"Blue means it's healthy," said Trove. "According to Benjamin. Speaking of which, I ought to formally introduce you," he continued as Francis returned to his starting point. "Ben, this is Francis Paige; he's joining us here on the Pantheon. Francis, meet Benjamin Thoroughgood. He's our Volum caretaker, and he does a rather fine job of it. Though he ought to leave the room a little more often," he added, looking sideways at the man.

"I'm studying," Benjamin answered.

"You didn't want to stretch your legs at the *Eden*?"

"Studying takes no pause."

"And when was the last time you ate? I haven't seen you in the canteen in days."

"Samuel has been bringing my meals down for me." Now Benjamin was starting to sound irate. "Are you finished? I've work to do."

"Yes, yes," Trove said. He looked back at Francis. "Let's be on our way."

They exited the room with a goodbye that sounded rather cursory from Benjamin. Then the door was closed and they were making their way back up the corridor.

"He's a strange one," Trove said. "Spends all his time with that thing. His interest is rather perverse, if you ask me."

"Do all ships have one of those things?"

"As far as I'm aware. Some have several, and the ports, like the one we picked you up from, have dozens. Likely hundreds, in the case of the *Eden*."

Another nod, but Francis said no more. His interest had been piqued, but now it fell away, leaving him with another reminder of how he had come to be here, and how he had been robbed of what could have been his only ride home.

4

Francis was allowed to skip lunch. He knew he was hungry; it had been well over twenty-four hours since he last ate. But his stomach felt like it had left him entirely, and he wanted to be alone. Instead he made his way to the library, where he first sat in silence, then stared at the bookcases.

His mother, father ... He wondered what they were thinking now. How they felt, to wake up in the morning and find him still not home. How they would feel as the days stretched into weeks, and their son didn't return. Vanished, without a trace.

"Hi."

Francis jerked. A tall, thin woman stood in the entryway, black hair tied back. He had seen her before; the one who'd stopped in the *Eden's* parking bay to ask Ruby for instructions. Francis groped for her name, but couldn't find it.

"You're Francis, right?"

"Yeah."

"I'm Natasha." She came in, just one step, and leaned against the wall with her arms folded. She smiled slightly.

Francis turned away. His eyes roved over the spines of the books on the shelves in front of him. Most were old, bound in leather. The lettering on some had been worn off.

"I don't presume to know what you're feeling," said Natasha, "but it's okay. To be scared. Angry. You have every right."

"Good," Francis muttered. "I should hope so."

"But if you ever want to talk, I'll listen."

Silence.

"No pressure. Give it some thought, hm?"

Francis nodded minutely.

Natasha lingered a moment longer, then he heard her feet as she pivoted to leave.

He turned. "What do you do here?" he asked.

She paused, came back over the threshold, then sat carefully in one of the chairs.

"I'm navigation leader."

"You fly the ship?"

"Hah. Sort of. Actually, mostly I tell two people at computer consoles what buttons to push, as well as keeping tabs on

Benjamin." She grinned. "I hear you met him today."

"Yeah."

"What did you think of him?"

"He was … interesting."

Natasha laughed. "Very tactful answer. That's not how most put it. Between you and me," she said in a lower voice, leaning forward, "there's at least one person on this ship that thinks he's rather *inclined* toward that thing, if you catch my drift."

Oh God.

The woman must have caught the horror on Francis's face, as she leaned back and laughed again. "Pay me no heed. No, Benjamin just likes to study it. For some reason the thing fascinates him. Haven't a clue why." She paused as if considering, then waved to the other seat. "You can sit down if you like."

Francis hesitated. He shook his head. "Thanks."

"Not a problem." Natasha's eyes swept the room, not at all disconcerted by the silence. "Find anything interesting to read?"

"No. I was just thinking, I guess."

"Ah. Well, I shall leave you to it." She stood. "It was nice talking to you, Francis." At the door, she paused and looked back. "I'll listen if you need it."

And with that, she was gone.

Modicum

(Chapter Five)

1

It was either the rumble of his stomach or the knock at the door that woke Francis the next morning, though he couldn't be sure which. Probably the former, he thought as he climbed out of bed and trudged to the door, as there was a definite vacuum in his midsection. No wonder; he'd skipped dinner last night too, and even though sitting around in a funk was hardly a tiresome activity, it was now almost forty-eight hours since the meagre breakfast he'd been given during his brief stint at Equity.

"Good morning," Trove greeted. He was, once again, alone. "Making good use of the pyjamas, I see."

Francis had been given a few sets of clothes, these striped flannel pyjamas included. They didn't fit particularly well, but it was better than spending the rest of his life in the same outfit.

"Hi," Francis said.

"Breakfast is being served in the canteen. Miss Celeste thought it best I collect you, given you skipped your meals yesterday."

A sour taste crept into Francis's mouth. He thought of declining the invitation, but as if on cue his stomach rumbled loudly, and he thought better of it. Depressed and stranded, yes, but that didn't mean he had to go hungry too.

"I need to change," Francis mumbled, casting a look back at his wardrobe. "Will you wait?"

"I shall be just up the corridor."

Pushing the door closed and then crossing to the wardrobe,

Francis opened the right-hand door. No sense opening both: there weren't enough sets of second-hand clothing to fill it out.

He stripped off and changed into a pair of black trousers that were easily a size too big, as well as a plain white t-shirt that was slightly more snug. Even so, when he looked in the mirror he tamped down a sigh. Almost everyone on board was used to some kind of manual labour, had muscles. Francis wasn't much different than Celeste's initial assessment—*"He looks like he weighs all of one-fifty soaking wet."*

He belted up the trousers and tucked the shirt in, but didn't look much better. For a while he fussed, wondered about just wearing his regular clothes again, but finally decided against it. His stomach was complaining noisily, and now he'd decided to eat, he realised just how hungry he was.

Leaving the room, he met Trove several metres down the corridor, where he stood poring over a sheet on that ever-present clipboard.

"Aha," he said, tucking it back under his arm as Francis approached. "You look like one of the team now."

If Trove was expecting a smile or something, he didn't get one. But it didn't matter, as he said, "This way," and headed up the corridor, Francis keeping pace in silence beside him.

The canteen was one of the larger rooms on the middle deck. Francis had been shown it during his tour yesterday, but then it was empty. Now it looked practically heaving: there were at least a dozen people here—how many people were aboard this ship? Seventeen, had Trove said?—most of them at square tables (bolted down, of course, along with the chairs), the rest queuing at the serving station by the near wall.

"I'm afraid our stocks are rather low at present," said Trove as he ushered Francis into the queue and handed over a tray from the nearby stack. He placed a bowl and spoon down for him, then assembled his own. "We're due to arrive at the next port in a few days, but until then pickings are slim."

He was right: all that was on offer was a somewhat grey vat of porridge. Standing over it, clutching a spattered ladle, was one of the biggest men Francis had ever seen. An apron was tied about his enormous frame, dwarfed in comparison to the man. And his face … well. There was no polite way about it: this man looked *slow*.

"Good morning, Samuel," Trove said when he and Francis reached the front of the queue.

The cook grunted. He gestured at Francis, who hesitated a moment and then extended his tray. Samuel dunked the ladle, then tipped it unceremoniously into Francis's bowl, before waving him aside to do the same for Trove.

"Don't mind him," Trove said as they moved for the nearest empty table. "Perfectly friendly man."

"Mm," was all Francis replied with.

Sitting down, Francis considered the porridge. He'd been hungry not minutes ago, but now, faced with this stodgy mess …

Then his stomach rumbled again, and he thought he'd better tuck in regardless.

He took a taste—

"Yes," Trove said with a knowing look. "Leaves a little to be desired, doesn't it?"

Francis chewed, slow, and then swallowed. Maybe he wasn't hungry after all.

"Is this all you have?"

"For now, I regret. I'm not particularly enamoured by it either." Trove gave his bowl a distasteful look. "Normally breakfast would be a little more colourful; beans, scrambled eggs, toast. A little more flavoursome, too." He spooned a bite into his mouth, considered, swallowed and then added, "Marginally."

They ate in relative quiet. Now and again someone would pass and say a hello to Trove or Francis, and after they were gone Trove would remind Francis of whether or not he'd met them, and who they were: "That's Mikhail; he's a general workhand. Usually on weapons, but since picking you up he's been repairing the decking." Or: "Sia Cowell; she's one of our technicians; spends most of her time in the control centre." Or: "Vala and Stefan. They're the Pantheon's resident couple."

By the time they were almost finished, the canteen was only half as full as it had been when they entered. Francis glanced about, trying to find the few faces he might recognise. No sign of that Benjamin fellow, and Natasha had already left.

There was no sign of Celeste, either.

"Morning, troops."

— never mind.

Ruby sat down with a tray of her own, smiling brightly. Francis gave her a cursory glance, then resumed fiddling with his spoon and the last dregs of his lukewarm breakfast. Probably for the best; glaring this early was surely considered impolite.

"Any news?" Ruby asked.

"Nothing particularly noteworthy," said Trove, checklist already in front of him. "We're flying a little low this morning, through a cloud formation, though Miss Brady assures me we should be clear shortly. And a power surge disrupted one of the condensers last night, but Peters corrected the fault and everything continues to run smoothly."

Ruby tutted. "Same battery?"

"That's right."

"We really ought to get that replaced."

"We had hoped to schedule maintenance at the *Eden* if we had time—but we didn't."

Ruby paused, spoon midway to her lips. She frowned. "No, we didn't." She chewed slowly, then turned to Francis. "And are you settling in?"

He glanced at her and shrugged before returning to his bowl.

"I expect those clothes aren't quite a perfect fit," Ruby continued. "Trove, would you see if you can free up some time in Vala's schedule?" To Francis she said, "Vala is the ship's seamstress, among other things. If you give her your measurements, she'll be able to take those clothes in for you properly."

Francis shrugged again. "Okay."

There was a moment of awkward silence.

An alarm's wail broke it, and a fraction of a second later—

Francis was tossed forward into the table as something boomed against the ship. Bowls and trays scattered, painting wet grey streaks across the table, floor—clothes—

Two more explosions juddered the ship.

The chatter in the canteen had dissipated. The world spun, then Francis was being pulled to his feet. Men and women were quickly moving into action, Ruby at the fore, issuing commands as the room emptied. It was she who had hold of Francis now, dragging him up by the wrist. Above everything, that alarm still sounded.

"Are you okay?" Ruby asked.

"I—"

They were moving now, out through the door, and Francis had to concentrate to get his feet to keep up. On Ruby's other side, Trove looked just as harried as he half-ran to keep pace, one hand plastered to the top of his head.

"What's happening?" Francis gasped.

Ruby glanced at him sidelong. Her mouth was set into a hard line. "We're under attack."

2

Every workstation in the control room was manned. Ruby released Francis by the door, then strode to the main display. Chatter filled the room as technicians gave reports.

"What happened?" Ruby asked.

"Not sure," said Sia. "Cameras four through six are all down for the count; damaged in the attack." She brought up the displays and cycled through, but there was nothing: not even static.

"What about before they were taken offline?"

"Camera five caught something black; a cannonball, I'd guess." A blurry still cycled onto her display, a black streak cut in a sea of white. "It only lasted a moment, and cloud cover is too dense to see anything else."

Fantastic; so now they were operating half-blind.

Another boom rocked the ship. Ruby clutched the back of Sia's chair, rooting herself to her feet until the vibration passed.

"Natasha," Ruby said, moving to the navigation leader, who was perched on a station of her own.

"Aye, Captain," she answered without looking up.

"I need the ship spun around. Direct all thrust into the spin, and then begin to climb. They're firing into our blind spot; I want cameras one through three focussed on the direction their shots are coming from."

"Got it."

"What if we lose those cameras too?" Sia asked.

Ruby didn't answer. Instead she returned to the door, and Francis, where he stood gripping the frame, eyes wide and panicked.

"You're going to want to hold tight."

Francis opened his mouth to speak, but didn't get a chance. The ship lurched around in a tight half-circle. His stomach felt like it might break through one side of his ribcage—

Then it was over and the ship began to rise.

Ruby shot Francis a glance. He looked positively green. Trove didn't look much better.

She strode back to the main console.

"Cameras one through three; on screen."

The main display flipped from diagnostics to the camera feeds. Right now there was nothing but white on each, swirling in the Pantheon's wake.

Ruby waited, watching.

Something streaked out of the abyss on camera three. It was visible for half an instant, and then two things happened: the ship rocked from the booming impact, on the other side now, and the feed went black.

"Cut it loose," Ruby instructed. A moment later, only cameras one and two remained on display. Toward the back of the room, she said, "Stefan, status on the portside cannons."

"Loaded and operational."

"Fire a volley of shots on my mark. Mark."

Thunder rumbled, and six cannons unloaded into the cloud.

"Mark."

Again.

"Mark."

And again.

"Cannons empty," Stefan said.

"Radio Mikhail and the others; I want them reloaded post-haste."

"Aye, Captain."

Turning back to the main console, Ruby said, "Diagnostic report."

This time the camera feeds remained, but Sia's display cycled through to a schematic of the entire ship. A number of sections were marked in amber, and text scrolled madly along the right-hand side of the screen.

"Battery One has failed; condensers have lost power. Re-route?"

"Not yet."

Another explosion rocked the ship, same direction as before. Static flickered on camera two, but its image held.

One of the amber lights on Sia's display blinked to red. "Hull has been split," she said.

Shit. Ruby spun. "Stefan: mark."

The cannons rumbled again.

Ruby opened her mouth to say something else, but Sia cried, "Captain!"

The feeds on the screen had changed: swirls of white parted, and through the gulf surged a black ship, half the Pantheon's size, twisting as it came. One of its fins was missing entirely, and great holes were torn in its wooden exterior, revealing blackened steel beneath, and in one place a great maw-like tear. A name was printed along the side in fat white letters: *MODICUM*, the bottom of the last M missing.

The cameras went dark. A shearing noise filled the air.

The room exploded into more chatter than ever: instructions and reports and radioed commands.

"We're being boarded!" someone shouted.

Ruby was already moving. "Natasha, cease all movement. I don't want to risk further damage to the ship if we're pushing in opposite directions."

"On it."

"Stefan, radio Mikhail. Inform his team of what's happening and get them up on deck."

"Yes, Captain."

"Sia, Amelie, put as much of the ship into lockdown as you can, leaving clear routes for us to get topside."

Two voices chorused: "Aye."

Ruby strode across the room.

"Awaiting orders," Trove said.

"Ensure things move smoothly," Ruby instructed.

Trove nodded, saluted, and was out the door.

That just left one person: Francis, whose terrified eyes roved the chaotic room. He still clung to the door frame as if expecting another explosion to rock the ship at any moment.

"Francis," Ruby said. His eyes fixed onto her, all whites. "You're coming with me."

3

"Where are we going?"

They were moving up the stairs to the upper deck, Ruby at a march, Francis hurrying along behind. Not that he had much choice in the matter: once again his wrist found itself clamped in her hand.

"You're about to get a real taste of what being a part of my crew is like," she said. And was that *brightness* in her voice? Apparently they were about to be boarded, and she was *cheerful*?

"I don't—" Francis started, but didn't finish; Ruby jerked him around a corner. Before he could catch his breath, they forked again into a room Trove had pointed out yesterday; storage.

Ruby deposited Francis by the door. Rubbing his wrist, Francis huffed for breath and took the place in. Greenish-grey metal lockers of various sizes filled the small space. A thin bench split it into two aisles.

"What's—"

"Aha!" Ruby withdrew something long from the locker she'd been sifting through. Beaming, she returned to Francis and swung it around his waist before he could shift.

"Hey!"

"Hold still," she cajoled.

"What are you doing?"

Evidently the thing she'd removed was attached to a belt, as she buckled it up as tight as it would go, then shuffled it from side to side with her hands. "Is that comfortable?"

Taking a backward step, she sized him up and grinned again. "Perfect. Your sword, Francis."

If his mouth could drop any further, it did then. "*What*?" Staring down, he saw it: the belt, and affixed on his left, a sheath from which protruded *the handle of a fucking sword*! "No!" His fingers pried at the buckle.

Ruby caught him. "Come on, we had to kit you out sometime." His wrist back in her hand, she exited the room, dragging him along behind.

"Stop!" Francis shouted. He pulled back, free hand desperately fiddling with the belt. "Wait, *stop*!"

Ruby paused. "What?"

Before he could speak, a voice shouted from up ahead: "Captain?"

Ruby pivoted, and Francis stared behind her. The ladder topside stood maybe half a dozen metres ahead, an uneven circle of light cast about its foot. Through the open porthole in the ceiling a head was visible.

"Mikhail?"

"There's something you need to see."

Ruby stepped forward, and Francis thought about just darting back—but she had his wrist, of course she did, and he was jerked along next to her, feet protesting before turning the stumble into the best walk he could manage.

"What is it?" Ruby asked. "How many are there?"

Mikhail pulled a face. "Nothing like that. It's … kind of hard to explain."

"Well, do your best."

"It's the ship itself. Huge parts of it—they're *missing*."

4

Ruby stared. For a long time, she wasn't really sure what she was looking at, because she had never seen anything quite like *this*.

The Modicum was a wreck. No, worse. The full front third of the topside deck was gone. Not just the wooden decking itself, but the steel beneath. Around the edges of the great, uneven hole she could just see it peering out in places, edges like frayed paper.

The Modicum's first level was visible underneath, but that was also incomplete. Rooms were sliced open, the ceiling and some of the walls missing, and the floor itself had been split apart, so that extra holes stared down into a blacker abyss below. Somewhere a light flickered, but its glow was brief and feeble.

"What happened here?" Ruby asked, but no one answered.

A crowd had gathered upon the Pantheon, by the rails, staring. They had expected the Modicum's crew to surge onto their ship, but so far no one had come. Were it not for the shots fired, this might have been a ghost ship.

After all, who let their ship degenerate into *this*?

Ruby allowed herself to take it in a moment longer, then gave a resolute nod. Turning to her crew, she said, "Right, people. No one has boarded us, so we're boarding them. Two teams; half with me, the rest led by Mikhail." He nodded at that. "This is SkyHugger-class, but it's small: two decks at most. We'll take the upper level;

Mikhail, you take lower. Encounter any resistance, you know what to do.

"Take care. Whatever happened here, this ship is clearly unstable. Be careful with your footing, and above all, remain aware at all times. *Someone* is on board, and I'm not about to fall into any traps."

A chorus: "Aye, Captain."

As the groups arranged themselves, Ruby stepped around the cluster. Francis was sat against the Pantheon's closest fin. His eyes were closed, and he cradled his legs. He looked pale.

"You're with me," Ruby said, crouching beside him. When he didn't look up, she continued, "We're going to look around, maybe salvage some supplies."

Still he didn't answer. Ruby waited, her lips pressing into a thin frown, before—

"Hey!" Francis cried, as she grabbed his wrists and jerked him to his feet.

"Relax," she simply said, and then turned and pulled him across the deck.

The crew had split into two teams now. Ruby's comprised Evans and Natasha. She gave them both a nod as they stood at attention.

"I want this to be a clean sweep," said Ruby. "Check every door, every corner. Deal with resistance as and when.

"Stick by me," she said to Francis. The only response he gave was a panicked look. "You're safe with us," she reminded him. Not that he looked convinced.

Mikhail took his team over the edge first, walking carefully across the small amount of decking the Modicum still possessed. Ruby watched as they moved, searching for the best point of entry; then Mikhail ordered them in one by one as they dropped down, first to one level, then to the level below.

Ruby listened. If anyone was hidden in wait, there would surely be a noise, a cry—but no sounds of battle came, and after a minute she gave her group a nod. "Okay. Let's go."

Evans climbed over first. Natasha gave Francis a curious look, then nodded at her captain and was over a moment later.

"Are you ready?" Ruby asked.

Francis gritted his teeth. He kept his eyes clasped tight.

"You just lift your leg up and over the railing," Ruby said. "Can you do that?"

He opened his eyes. For one moment they looked wild, before he slammed them shut and shook his head.

"Why not?"

"Because we're *in the air*," he gasped.

"Well, yes. So what's the worry?"

"What if I *fall*?"

"Ah. Don't you worry about that," Ruby said. "You're with me!"

"You almost got me shot."

Ruby waved it off. "'Almost' and 'did' are worlds apart. Now come on; we haven't got all day. We'll even do it together."

She stepped up to the rail, hand clamped tight on Francis's arm. He moaned, but a little tug from Ruby was all it took for him to edge forward.

"That's it. Now, lift up your left leg—come on, lift it up— higher—and move it over the railing."

He did as instructed, eyes closed the whole time. Ruby watched as he grimaced, moved to place his foot—and floundered when it didn't meet floor. He tumbled forward and let out a gasp; she tightened her grip on him, and his foot made contact with the Modicum's deck.

"There we go," she said. "That wasn't so bad, was it?"

"I—I thought I was falling."

Ruby suppressed a smile. "You're safe. Now: the other one."

5

"Easy," Ruby muttered, edging around a hole in the floor.

They were moving through the Modicum's upper deck, having

slipped down in roughly the same spot as Mikhail's team. So far they had heard and encountered nothing.

The Modicum was even worse on the inside. Enormous sections of decking and panelling were just *gone*, ripped up entirely. The steel hull was visible in some of these places, but in others it was missing, the edges of these wounds discoloured. At first Ruby had thought it corrosion, but this wasn't rust. The closer she looked, the more she thought it matched her initial assessment: the hull had frayed like paper. Once she moved to touch it, but changed her mind and withdrew her hand.

The rooms so far had been empty, and Ruby wasn't surprised. But still, there was something wrong. *Someone* was on the ship, she knew; someone had fired upon the Pantheon. The question was, where?

She brought her wrist to her mouth, tapped on the communicator, and opened a radio channel to Mikhail. "Report."

"Empty down here," he said. "There are a lot of holes. But we've found a supply cupboard; could restock."

"Good. Keep me posted." Ruby thumbed the channel off.

This corridor was curved, and holes wended across the floor. In one place they had almost had to turn around where a maw had half-eaten it and a great chunk of the right-hand wall. Still, it had felt stable enough—a little bit of give, but the whole place had that—and so they'd crossed anyway.

A door loomed ahead, on the right. Ruby mentally checked the ship's layout, worked out just how far they'd come.

Natasha had done the same, apparently, as from behind she muttered, "Control centre?"

"One way to find out."

They reached the door. Ruby pulled Francis close to her. His breathing had evened out somewhat, but he was still edgy, and in the dim, flickering lights she could see he remained pale.

"On my mark," she whispered. "One, two: mark."

Evans thrust open the door, then stormed inside, pistol drawn. Natasha was in a moment later, and Ruby followed, pulling

Francis.

This was the control centre, or once had been. Terminals were busted, most of them, and that same mottled fraying had crawled over several of the workstations, exposing circuitry. An amber light pulsed unsteadily. And in one corner—

"*Get off my ship!*"

The man they faced was haggard. His complexion was sallow. The skin of his face looked taut, unhealthily so, and uneven facial hair sprouted in curled brown tufts. Even in the dull light, Ruby could tell his eyes had yellowed in the corners. The irises were blue, but faint, barely half a shade darker than the whites, so his pupils seemed frighteningly dark—and small.

"Who are you?" Ruby demanded.

He didn't answer. His eyes darted madly from one to the other, and his mouth worked, but no sound came out.

"I said, who are you?"

— and then he lifted a gun.

Hands flew to weapons, bodies pressed low. Someone let out a terrified gasp—Francis, of course—and Ruby stepped across his body, her sword poised.

"S'empty," the man said. "See!" He pointed it skyward and pulled the trigger, but only a hollow click came. "Empty!" Grinning, he dropped it. "S'all I've got."

Ruby didn't relax. "Who are you?"

"Captain. Of this ship." The last word was long, drawn out. He pressed on the top of the workstation closest, lifted himself onto unsteady legs. "Who are *you*?"

"That's irrelevant," said Ruby.

The man's eyes roved. His pupils were so tiny, even in the low light.

"Why did you fire upon my ship?" Ruby demanded.

He grinned again, a madman's leer, and took a forward step. Ruby felt Francis press backward behind her.

This captain's whole body was bony, she saw now. How had he become so malnourished? And—

"Where are your crew?" she asked.

"Hah! Shot 'em." He leaned against the wall, sideways. A look came across his face, almost—reminiscent?

Ruby opened her mouth to ask why, but he wasn't finished.

"Had to. They'd got it. All of 'em." A momentary pause. "Well, not *all*. Some of them mighta fallen." He sighed, a strangely melancholic sound, before crossing his arms and then letting them drop unceremoniously to his sides. His eyes had fallen to the floor, but now they came up to Ruby again, and a light seemed to click on inside them. "You're alive."

She was silent.

"I thought," the loon began, but let the sentence trail off. Finally he said, "Wrong."

"Is there anyone else aboard this ship?"

"Hah! Me—the Volum. No one else. I told you; they're all dead. Shot 'em."

Quiet. Then Ruby said, "I see."

Without warning, she crossed to the deranged man.

"You—" he began, but Ruby cut across.

"You shall not fire upon my ship again."

She thrust her sword forward in one easy motion. There was a horrible *shick* sound as it went right through the man's chest, halfway to the hilt. Francis gasped, pedalled backward into a wall as his vision tunnelled—and then Ruby pulled it free with that same horrifying sound.

The man held still for a moment, expressionless—and then crumpled to the floor.

6

The Modicum turned out to be the answer to all of Ruby's needs: the pantry was almost full, which meant they no longer needed to check into *The Oft-Trodden Footpath*. Beyond that, there were further items Ruby's crew could salvage: medical supplies, filters for the condensers, maintenance equipment, pellets for the Volum.

Over the course of the next few hours, these things were sifted through by the Pantheon's crew, and anything deemed useful was taken back onto their ship.

The captain's words proved true: there was not a soul on board the Modicum. No bodies remained, either; if the crazed captain had shot every person on his ship then he had disposed of the corpses.

Ruby stood now in what had once been the captain's quarters. The room was somewhat smaller than her own, and just as holey as the rest of the ship. It was unruly, too; the few possessions in here were littered all over the place, and the desk was almost completely covered in ink. The empty jar sat in a fat black stain on the floor, dried long ago.

There was very little in here of value. A single jar remained unbroken on a shelf, the glass murky. A label was stuck to it but the writing had faded to illegibility. Ruby considered taking it; maybe someone could identify its contents. But she changed her mind and moved on.

The bed was messy, stained. She flicked the cover off by the tiniest edge of material pinched in her thumb and forefinger, careful not to touch it. The sheet beneath was worse. She did the same with the pillow, tossing it aside, and found—

A book. A diary, by the looks. Carefully, she stooped and picked it up, flicking through its pages.

Nothing interesting. Most entries were cursory, filled out for no reason other than for something to do at the end of a day.

But—

She paused, flicked backward a page. The writing terminated abruptly. It had turned into a scrawl—the scrawl of a madman?

The last full entry was brief; it recanted his shooting someone named Malloy, then tossing the body overboard. The last sentence had been started but not finished: '*Of all the places, in all the*'

Four blank lines followed. Then came two words, and beneath, two numbers: the final notes this man had penned.

'*Ghost Armada*'. And below—co-ordinates?

Ruby frowned. She fell down into the seat by the desk and stared at the page. Ghost Armada. That sounded ... familiar. A legend? Probably. Almost definitely, given the word 'ghost'.

Had the Modicum been searching for it? Had that been what drove the captain mad?

She bit her lip and puzzled. "The Ghost Armada," she muttered to the empty room. "Hm."

Letter

(Chapter Six)

1

Natasha had just finished eating as Trove stepped into the canteen—alone. She frowned. Rising from her table, she weaved through the seats with her tray and empty plate, arriving beside the man.

"You're by yourself," she said, stowing the tray in the nearby rack.

"Mr Paige isn't hungry," Trove answered. "I expect you'll find him in the library, if you're looking."

"Ah. Well. Thank you, Trove." Natasha gave a nod, which Trove returned, and then departed.

She stopped by her quarters first, and then headed for the library. True to Trove's word, there was Francis: sat on one of the plush seats, staring through the floor. There was a book on his lap, but the pages had fanned upward, forgotten.

"Evening," Natasha said.

Francis looked up. "Hi."

She sat down opposite. "How are you feeling?"

He shrugged. "Fine."

"You didn't seem fine."

For a moment he was silent, then said: "When? When your captain strapped a sword to my side? When she forced me onto that other ship with her?" He faltered, and his mouth worked wordlessly for a second. "When she—she stabbed that man?"

Natasha waited for him to go on. When it was clear he wouldn't, she said calmly, "All of those times. And before, and since."

"Hah. Well, what a surprise." He smirked to himself, an unfunny sound, and then glanced up at Natasha. Their eyes met for a second before he dropped them. "I'm not cut out for this."

"No one ever said you were."

"*She* seems to think so." He jabbed toward the doorway on 'she'. "She thinks I'd love to be thrown right in, to—to be given a sword and—and—"

"Why did you go along with it?"

"What?"

"The sword; coming topside; climbing onto the Modicum with us," said Natasha. "Why do it?"

"Because I had no choice."

"There's always a choice. Ruby doesn't force anyone."

"*Hah.*"

Natasha was quiet for a moment. Then she reclined in the chair and looked down at the book in Francis's lap. "What're you reading?"

He folded it over and flashed Natasha the cover; a book of legends she had glanced through once or twice before. "Wasn't really reading it," he said. "You can have it if you want."

"No, thanks. Actually, I have something for you."

Francis looked at her again, at what she carried. It was a book, cover brown leather, unmarred.

"I've already got a book," he said.

"Do you have a diary?"

"What?"

Natasha flipped it open. The pages were blank. "It's a diary. You know what they say; writing can be therapeutic. Gives you a chance to get your feelings out."

Francis considered. Finally, he looked away, back through the floor. "What's the point." It wasn't a question.

"Just think about it." Natasha placed it down on the table between them, pushed it an inch or so across, and rose. "It might help. And if not, you're only out some time."

He didn't reply, so she headed for the door.

"She *killed* him," Francis whispered.

Natasha paused. Turned. Met his eyes.

"She *killed* that man. And all those people at the *Eden*. And she's your *leader*?"

"Ruby is a good person."

"Is she?" Francis asked. "Do good people kill?"

Natasha nodded. "Up here, they do," she said quietly.

Silence … and then she turned and was gone.

2

The clock said it was well past nine when Francis finally extracted himself from the library. That meant most of the crew would have retired to their quarters. Good; he didn't much fancy making small talk.

For a second he thought about just leaving the diary on the table, where it had sat untouched for hours. But he hesitated just an instant, and that instant was enough to convince him to pick it up. Natasha was right; it could be therapeutic. Or pointless. Francis wasn't sure which.

His door shut and locked, he sat down on his bed, heaved a sigh, and considered the book. It was heavy, though not very thick. And new: a waxy sheen covered the leather. The pages were thicker than regular paper, and faintly yellow.

Francis pondered. What would he write? It had been three days since being kidnapped. Three days stranded up here, with no way down.

Well. No way down that hadn't been blown up by his red-haired 'saviour'.

What would his parents have thought? Had they noticed during the night? He'd tried to make some commotion as his captors snatched him out of bed, but a hand was clamped over his mouth barely before he could fully awake—and those men, heavyset though they were, had been as stealthy as cats.

No, his parents wouldn't have known until he was late for breakfast. Maybe even later; they might've thought he was having a lay-in. It might not have been until early afternoon that his father knocked on his door, asking if he was up, if everything was all right.

And when they found the room empty—what then? Would they have known something had happened? Maybe they would simply think Francis had gone out early, would be back late.

Maybe they wouldn't have started to worry until the next day.

And now …

Francis closed his eyes and tried to wish the thought away. He couldn't bear the image of their stricken faces as they wondered what had happened, set out searching for him.

How long would they look?

And when they didn't find him—when would they give up?

Maybe they'd think he'd run away from home.

That thought was like a punch to the stomach.

"Stop it," Francis muttered. "Just … stop it."

He balled up his fists, as if he could squeeze and strangle everything running through his head. Then he dropped them to his lap.

They met leather.

The diary.

What a stupid thing to give him. What was the point in getting his thoughts down? This book, it wasn't a person—not a person that mattered. Not someone he could speak to; he would simply be communicating with himself—

He paused. Stared.

He could … write a letter. Could write something to his parents, print their address on it, and drop it over the side of the ship. He had no idea where it would land, but someone would surely find it. That someone would pass it on.

He could tell them that he was okay.

They could never write back, but …

Climbing to his feet, Francis crossed the small space to the desk and pulled open the single drawer. Only two things were inside, but they were exactly what he needed: a bottle of ink, and a pen. Pulling them out and furiously uncapping the bottle, he opened the book to the first page, dipped the end of the pen, and began to write as fast as he could.

Mum, Dad;

This is Francis. I don't know if this will reach you, but I'll pray with all that I have it will.

I was kidnapped. The man who took me was someone called Rhod Stein, but I think he may be dead now. I was stolen to be sold as a worker, and the person that took me, a woman called Ruby Celeste, she blew everything up.

I'm not down there anymore. Now I'm stuck on some kind of flying ship. Oh God, I'm so scared—yesterday we were attacked and the captain forced a sword onto me. She killed people! Right in front of me!

I don't know how to get home. I don't know if I <u>can</u> get home. But if I can find a way, I will. I promise.

<u>I didn't run away.</u>

*<u>**I love you.**</u> I miss you.*

Francis Paige

A dim part of him was aware that his face was hot and wet, and the ink had bled in one spot where a tear had fallen.

He tore out the page carefully, read it one final time, then folded it into the smallest square he could. On the outside he wrote the address, then unfolded it and printed it along the bottom in block capitals before refolding.

This had to work. It just had to. He had to let them know that he was okay.

There was just the simple matter of getting it to them.

3

Francis unlocked his door, slow and careful. Suddenly he felt almost guilty, as if he were sneaking about.

"Don't be stupid," he chided himself. But still, the feeling remained.

The corridor was empty as he stepped out. Nonetheless, he slunk, keeping his footfalls as light as possible lest anyone hear and throw a door open.

No one did.

He passed the storage room. The door was closed; good. He had deposited his belt and sword in there the moment he returned to the Pantheon, just tossing them down into a corner before practically fleeing to the confines of his room. Dully, he wondered if anyone had found it yet, stowed it once more into the locker it had come from.

Then he was past it, and up ahead loomed the ladder topside.

He stood at it and paused.

"Come on," he muttered.

He extended one hand, placed it on a rung; did the same with the other, reaching one rung higher. One foot—

He froze. Because once he was out, it meant standing at the edge of the ship, looking out into the abyss.

"Get a grip," he told himself. "Just do it."

Five seconds went by; six, seven …

"Come on!"

He shifted, and the letter in his pocket brushed against his leg.

That was enough to wheel him into motion. With a momentary glance backward, he brought himself onto the ladder and climbed; two rungs, three, four …

The topside hatch was closed, and Francis stopped to look. A wheel stood in its centre, so with one hand he gripped it tight and tugged. Some part of him was convinced it wouldn't move—*"He looks like he weighs all of one-fifty soaking wet"*—but mercifully it budged instantly. He rotated until it would spin no more, and then pushed it open.

The night air was cool, and still—or at least it was still here, inside the Volum's sphere of influence. What it was like further out, Francis didn't know.

Reaching skyward were the Pantheon's three fins, each pulsing gently with a subtle red glow from whatever covered them in intricate patterns. Beyond, the sky was alive with hundreds, perhaps thousands, of stars. A great streak that had the vaguest hint of plum colour was painted to Francis's right.

"Admire it later," he whispered. "Come on."

Taking care again that his steps were soft, he headed left across the deck. The first half-dozen metres were easy, but as the railing loomed closer his footsteps turned to a lurch. Three metres from the Pantheon's edge, he stopped entirely.

"Be a man! It's easy. Just take one step, then another."

He breathed deeply. In, out. In, out. In—one step. Out—another.

"That's it. Keep going."

In—left foot. Out—right. In—he froze.

"Almost there. Come on!"

For a full thirty seconds he stood, gasping in the air. He counted, said he'd go on three, then five, then ten, then thirty, and still he didn't move.

"Go!"

He jerked forward at his own instruction, crossed the last few steps, and grabbed the railing as hard as he could.

He breathed heavily. Continued to stare straight ahead.

He was here. Safe. No wind, nothing to push him overboard. He was safe.

Still, he didn't fancy hanging around. He dug into his pocket, fumbled past his room key, and withdrew the folded letter. Taking it out, he gave it one final look.

"Godspeed," he whispered.

Placing a kiss upon it, he extended his hand over the side and let it go.

He was about to turn on his heel when someone grabbed him. A gasp burst from his lips, and he teetered backward, away from the edge.

"Easy, cowboy," muttered a man. It was a voice Francis didn't recognise; certainly no one from this ship. "Who are you?"

"F-Francis Paige," he answered automatically.

"Ah. The stolen property."

"Who—"

"Don't ask questions." The man wheeled back, pulling Francis with him. Francis's legs obeyed without hesitation. "You know the layout of this ship?"

"Yes," Francis breathed.

"Good, good." There was a touch of a smile to the voice now. "Well then, Francis Paige, you're going to lead me to Ruby Celeste."

4

Francis was half-walked, half-dragged across the deck until they arrived at the open porthole.

"Now, Francis, I'm going to let you go. You're going to climb down that ladder, then turn up the corridor and wait. Understand?"

Francis nodded quickly.

"You will do exactly as instructed and no more. Don't think to raise an alarm; don't think to make a sound; don't think to do anything except what I just said. If you do …" He paused, and a half-second later Francis felt cold metal press against the side of his forehead. He jerked, gasped, but his assailant's grip was too tight to move.

"That's it." Smiling again, low and dangerous and terrifying. "Now, Francis Paige, go down the ladder."

The arm holding him vanished, and the barrel of the gun pulled away at the same moment as he was nudged forward. Francis almost lost his footing, almost gasped, cried out—but he stifled. No sound.

Resisting the urge to turn around, he squatted beside the

porthole, swung his legs onto a rung, and clambered down.

What if there was someone up the corridor? What if someone happened to be passing? Could he say something? Maybe Natasha, or Trove—

But the corridor was empty, he saw as he reached the bottom, and Francis was alone. Alone with an armed man ready to kill him at a moment's notice.

A soft *whump* sounded behind Francis, and a second later that arm had snaked back around him. No warning sound of feet upon rungs; one drop, plain and simple, and almost noiseless.

"You know where we're going?"

Francis nodded. "Yes."

"Good. Take us there. And don't try anything."

To emphasise the last, hard metal pressed against Francis's temple again.

"Walk."

He obeyed.

The journey to Ruby's quarters was short; just a case of following the corridor's curve. As they went, Francis wondered— would someone step out? Up ahead? Behind them? What then? And if not, what would this man do to Ruby? To Natasha, to Trove?

What would happen to Francis?

This man had referred to him as 'stolen property'. That meant he must have come from Rhod Stein, from the *Eden*. Did that mean Rhod had survived? And did that mean Francis had a way home after all?

"Are you going—" he began, but metal against his temple cut the words off.

"Quiet, cowboy."

On the right: one door, looming, now past, and then the door to Ruby's quarters.

"This is it," Francis breathed. He juddered to a halt, not entirely of his own accord. "Right here."

"Ruby Celeste's room."

"Yes."

"Good. Knock."

Francis lifted a hand. It quivered.

He knocked.

Quiet.

The door yawned open.

A shock of red hair.

"Francis—"

Two things happened, fast.

One: Francis was pushed hard to the side.

Two: a gunshot.

He hit the floor. A fraction of a second later, someone else did a few feet behind him.

Eyes fastened tight, he lay there, gasping, waiting.

Somewhere, a door opened. More than one. Voices. Mikhail was somewhere amidst the fray, Francis could hear, thundering up the corridor. One of the technicians—Amelie, he thought. And—

"Francis?"

Hands flew to his wrist, his neck, feeling for a pulse.

His eyelids flitted open.

Natasha: "You're okay."

"Is Ruby—" he started.

"Fine." She pulled him up to seated. Worry lines etched her forehead. Her eyes swept the hallway; Francis followed.

There, slumped against the wall, was a black-clad body. A gun lay a few feet from his hand. His head was hidden just out of view by someone's legs; the spray of claret and gore against the wall behind it was not. Francis paled, turned away.

Ruby stood in the doorway. Shell-shocked, she was ashen. Mikhail stood to one side, talking quickly. Ruby's answers came in one- and two-word sentences.

"Who—" Francis began. He swallowed, but his throat was dry and papery. "Who shot him?"

Natasha pointed.

Stood behind Ruby was Trove. A clipboard lay discarded by his feet, pages ruffled. Instead he grasped a pistol, its barrel still smoking gently from above his bone-white knuckles.

5

Ruby stared. Mikhail was talking in her ear, and there were voices all around in the corridor. She needed to focus, but all she could do was gaze at the dead man against the opposite wall, a wreck where his head had once been.

This man would have killed her, if not for Trove.

She blinked, turned. He was locked into position, weapon still poised in his grip.

"You can put the gun down now, Trove," she said, voice low.

His eyes moved to hers. As if waking, recognition dawned. He nodded, then stowed the pistol back within his coat. His movements were slow.

"Mikhail." She turned back. The wheels of her brain were in motion again now. She had been caught off-guard, but it was time to take charge. "Assemble into teams. I want a full sweep of the ship."

"Aye."

"Amelie. Sound the alarm, then put the ship into lockdown. You, Sia and Stefan are all on comms; open doors only when necessary to allow our scouts access."

"Yes, Captain."

"Natasha." The navigation leader snapped to a salute. "Take nav control; full thrust. Pick a direction and follow it; I don't care which. Just get us out of here."

Natasha nodded; she pivoted on her heel and then was gone.

"Francis."

He looked up, met Ruby's eyes. For once that guarded look didn't cross his face.

"I need to know what happened."

She expected for a second that he might not tell her, but his answer came with no delay: "I was up on deck and he just—just grabbed me."

Ruby frowned. "Up on deck?"

"Natasha gave me a diary. I thought I could write my parents a letter and drop it; maybe it might get to them."

"Oh." The word was softer, just slightly.

"He came up behind me."

"Did you hear him?"

Francis shook his head. "No."

"What then?"

"He asked who I was. I told him. Then he asked if I knew the layout of the ship, and told me to lead him to you." His mouth worked for a moment, before he finally said, "That's it."

Ruby gave the dead man a demure glance, then exchanged a look with Trove. Finally, she said to Francis, "It's late. The ship is in lockdown, so you won't get into your room. Why don't you go to the library? I'll send Natasha to keep you company when she's done."

Francis nodded. He seemed to hesitate a fraction of a second, then turned and disappeared up the corridor. Ruby watched him go.

"You don't think," Trove began.

Ruby waved the thought off. "No, I don't."

But as she wheeled into action, preparing to scour the ship for unexpected occupants, she pondered Trove's unasked question: had Francis had anything to do with the attack?

No, she didn't think so.

Though 'think' did leave some wiggle room for doubt.

6

It was well into the early hours of the morning that Natasha finally wandered into the library. For most of this time, Francis had been alone; now and again someone had come by, chatted with him (at him) before departing, but no one had stuck around.

"How're you holding up?" Natasha asked. She slumped down

into the free chair and leaned her head back.

"Fine," said Francis. "You?"

She pulled a tense smile. "Just super." Massaging the corners of her eyes, she let out a long sigh, then sat up straighter. "Sorry," she said. "The ship is somewhat chaotic right now."

"I can imagine." Not that Francis needed to. Sat across from her, he could see just how drawn she looked. Dark patches were starting to form beneath her eyes.

Speaking lower, Natasha said, "Are you sure you're okay? What happened out there?"

Francis told her the same he'd told Ruby. Natasha listened; she didn't ask questions, like Ruby had; merely sat and took the little information in. Only when he'd finished did she lean back in the seat, thoughtful, before finally saying, "And he didn't say who he was? Where he was from?"

"Nope. Just told me what to do and how to do it."

"I see."

"He … he called me 'stolen property'," Francis said. "Could Rhod have sent him?" When Natasha didn't say anything, he added, "You know … to take me back."

"It's possible," Natasha said slowly.

"So … so I could get home after all."

A pained expression crossed the nav leader's face. Fixing eyes with Francis, she held his gaze.

"Francis, that man was here for Ruby. He was here to kill her— and if you'd tripped up, it sounds very much to me like he would have killed you too. Maybe Rhod Stein did send him—if he's still alive, at any rate—but if that's the case, is that someone you really want to go back with? Someone who put a gun to your head and was willing to pull the trigger?

"Ruby is a good person," Natasha continued. "*We* are good *people*. I know you being stuck here isn't ideal, but hoping to go back to the man that ordered your kidnap in the first place, then sent an assassin to board this ship in the dead of night—it's not something you should wish for. If he took you back, do you really think he'd give you a ride home?"

Quiet.

"Ah; Miss Celeste said I'd find you here."

Natasha and Francis turned to the doorway. Mikhail stood, one hand resting on the frame. Casual; almost as if he hadn't been searching for more attackers these past few hours.

"Hello, Mikhail," Natasha said. "How did the search go?"

"Came up empty. Anyhow, ship's out of lockdown now. That means we can go back to our quarters. Thought I'd give you both the heads-up."

Natasha nodded. "Thanks." She suppressed a yawn, rose and stood, stretching her long body. "See you," she said to Francis, and then departed.

"How you feeling?" Mikhail asked.

Francis glanced at him, shrugged. "I'm okay. Thanks."

"You did well. Commendable, keeping your nerve. Lot of other folk would've screamed their heads off."

"Yeah, well, I suppose you keep zipped and follow instructions when there's a gun pointed at your head."

Mikhail smirked. "Maybe so, but still." He straightened. "Heading back to bed?"

"In a minute." Francis lifted the book that had been laying in his lap and gave it a little wave. "Just going to finish this page."

"All right. Take it easy."

Francis pretended to read as Mikhail loped off. Once the corridor was empty, he let his eyes stop trawling the page. His focus drifted.

Natasha's words replayed in his head. Had she been right? Was he so desperate for a ride home, any ride, that he thought Rhod Stein would take him back if he managed to return to the man's clutches?

He was torn. On the one hand, Rhod was the only person around for hundreds of miles that had the capability to take him home.

But on the other, he had sent someone to the Pantheon—or at

least it seemed that way—who was poised to kill Ruby. And then what? Would he have killed Francis too?

No matter how long Francis thought about it, no answers came.

Rhod Stein Receives a Call

(Chapter Seven)

1

Clean-up on *The Pharmacologist's Eden* was an enormous undertaking—though it felt less like 'clean-up' and more like 'reconstruct the entire damn thing with half the workforce and a bunch of know-all contractors, pissing through as much cash as possible'. Good thing Rhod had invested wisely, or this would've ruined him.

He'd rallied to keep the SkyPort operating. Most of the repairs were needed at the back end, he reasoned; no sense in ceasing trade for the whole of the *Eden* when the front half was still functional. But he'd been strongly advised against it; yes, that part of the *Eden* looked fine, but that didn't mean it wasn't unstable, particularly with the rear wall of storefronts either missing or dangerously contorted.

There was also the matter of power. Cables were constantly being disconnected and reconnected as debris was cleared. One minute they might be powered, the next most of the *Eden* could go dark.

Most of the larger pieces of rubble were gone now, including the remains of what had once been Rhod's office, but that meant no shortage of smaller pieces of wreckage. Rhod watched this clean-up op now, silent and brooding. Mostly contractors; too few faces Rhod recognised. Fleeing bastards.

God, how he hated those contractors. All he wanted was to run the port. Instead they'd been turning ships away for days. Fewer and fewer were arriving now; word was trickling elsewhere that Rhod Stein's *Eden* wasn't open to customers, but *was* open to a gentle breeze that flowed through the gaping wound in the SkyPort's side.

A click sounded at his belt. The radio. He lifted it off and pressed the transmitter.

"Stein."

"Call for you, sir."

"On my way."

Thumbing the radio off and clipping it back to his belt, he rose. He gave the contractors a final grimace, then lumbered in the direction of the nearest storefront and its phone.

2

The shop Rhod passed through was a fashion outlet. He breezed through aisles of clothing forged between clusters of circular racks, found the door to the staff office, and pushed through. Like Equity, it wasn't as clean and chic back here; there was a rather dilapidated look to the furniture, and a brown stain marred the carpet. Coffee, probably.

He hefted down into a chair behind a desk. There were two phones; lifting the nearest from the cradle, he waited, keyed in his code, and then pressed the number '1' for the waiting line.

"Took long enough," said a scratchy, weathered voice, with just a touch of glee.

Rhod grunted, "Imelda."

"Repairs nicely underway?"

"Quit the small-talk and get to it. What do you want? Did you find Celeste yet?"

Imelda smirked, a nasal sound even over the poor connection. "We're rather brash today, Rhod."

"Get to the point."

"There's been a little setback." The gleeful note to Imelda's voice was gone. Gripping the phone tighter, Rhod leaned forward.

"One of my men dropped onto the ship last night, but never reported back. We found his Pod empty, no sign of him."

"Celeste got him," Rhod muttered.

"Presumably."

"Your men are meant to be the best! What's happened since I last took out your services?"

"Don't give yourself a coronary, big man," said Imelda. "She got lucky, nothing else."

"Or your man isn't as good as you think—"

"Celeste got *lucky*," Imelda hissed. There was a brief pause, and when her voice returned she was calmer, more collected. "You'll have her head on a stick, and soon. The Pod's cams caught her ship disappearing; I have her vector."

"Maybe you ought to dispatch more next time. Just in case she gets *lucky* again."

"Oh, I will. I don't take kindly to the loss of any of my people. I assure you, Rhod, next time Celeste will have a whole group to contend with. We'll see if she gets lucky *then*."

The Pantheon, Redirected
(Chapter Eight)

1

The morning came far too early, Natasha thought as she trudged through the Pantheon to the canteen, even for someone accustomed to early mornings, late nights.

The cafeteria was empty. The ship's crew awoke at the same time, more or less; some of the techies worked night shifts, and wouldn't rise until the afternoon, but otherwise the majority of the workforce was in the process of getting up now. The excitement of the previous night must have had everyone working at less than full speed.

"Morning," Natasha said to Samuel. He nodded, then waved for her to extend her tray.

No porridge this morning: instead Natasha was treated to a single slice of poorly buttered toast (one side had received almost all of the spread, whereas the other was bone dry), a ladleful of beans, a scoop of diced mushrooms, and a fried egg, which split open and spilled runny yolk across the plate as Samuel deposited it.

Thank goodness for the Modicum, Natasha thought, perching down on a corner table. Yesterday hadn't been all bad.

She chewed slowly, thinking on the previous night. How was Francis doing? Perhaps she'd check in with him later, when she got a chance. Or maybe he'd arrive shortly, accompanied by Trove.

A trickle of people came over the next five minutes; Vala and

Stefan together, Stefan in need of a shave; then Herschel, who was followed closely by Mikhail; he grinned and said, "Sleep all right?" to Natasha as he passed, earning him the middle finger of Natasha's right hand.

As Natasha mopped up the last of the sauce from her beans with the dry end of her toast, Trove stepped in. She looked up for Francis, but Trove had come alone—and instead of heading to the serving station, he wove through the tables, moving directly for her.

"Howdy," Natasha said. "Pull up a pew."

Trove sat down. "Miss Brady."

"Feeling okay? You know, after last night."

"A little shaken, but none the worse for wear."

"Excellent."

"I have a request," Trove said. He flipped his clipboard onto the table and scrutinised the top page for a second. "Miss Celeste would like to re-route the ship."

"Oh?" Natasha popped the last corner of toast into her mouth, chewed, and swallowed. "I thought we were heading for the nearest SkyPort."

"We were," said Trove. "But the Modicum's stores plugged most of our holes, so the trip isn't necessary. And Miss Celeste wishes to go … somewhere else."

An eyebrow rose on Natasha's face. "You look troubled, Trove. What's up?"

He glanced around for listeners. But the cafeteria was now a hubbub, so no one was in danger of overhearing.

"I believe it to be something of a flight of fancy," he confided in a low voice. "During our encounter with the Modicum yesterday, Miss Celeste discovered a diary. In the back was a set of co-ordinates, and the words …" He glanced down at the clipboard as if checking what he had noted was correct, before finishing, "'Ghost Armada'."

"I see," Natasha said after a long pause.

"Nothing more than the deranged writings of a madman; at

least, that's what I think."

"Did you tell her so?"

"Of course."

"And she didn't listen."

Trove fixed Natasha with a look. "Have you met our captain?"

Natasha chewed her lip. She glanced down at the clipboard. Sure enough, there on the topmost sheet was exactly what Trove had said: the words 'Ghost Armada', printed in his tidy scrawl, and a set of co-ordinates. A question mark had been drawn and bracketed to one side of the paper.

"So she wants us to find it?"

Trove nodded. "I tried to talk her out of it, but ... Given the Modicum's wealth of stores, we really have no reason now to check into *The Oft-Trodden Footpath*. We've got enough to last us weeks."

"What about repairs? We're minus four of our cameras."

"I thought that, but no; they snatched several of the Modicum's before we left her yesterday. They'll be wired up today."

"First aid supplies? Maintenance?"

"No and no. As I said, the Modicum plugged our gaps; it even brought us up to surplus in some places. We've got no reason whatsoever to check into port for at least three weeks. Food is— *was*—our main concern, and the Modicum's cache was almost full of that."

Natasha nodded. "Well, at least you tried. So am I re-routing the ship today?"

"As soon as possible." Trove unclipped the sheaf of paper and handed it over. Natasha glanced over it, memorising its brief contents, and then folded it and slipped it into a pocket.

"I'll get to it in a moment, then." Drumming her hands, she glanced around the room. It really had filled out now. "No Francis?"

"I'll collect him in a moment; Miss Celeste thought this more pertinent."

"Fair enough. Any idea where our attacker came from?"

Trove shook his head. "The working cameras didn't catch anything. Miss Celeste suspects it was a specialised vehicle; something made for creeping. Whatever the case, I doubt we'll ever know now."

"I see. What happened to the body?"

"Darrel's running an autopsy to see if maybe we can find anything; identichips, a tracking device. Certainly nothing worthwhile was in his clothes; all he carried was his jumpsuit, gun and a knife."

They sat quietly for a few moments. Chatter filled the room. Surprisingly, despite last night's events, it was mostly idle. Only a few snippets of conversation met Natasha's ears about the attempted assassination; mostly people just talked about what their day's plans involved. Then again, that wasn't too much of a surprise; though word had almost surely travelled through the entire crew by now, Ruby usually called a meeting after big events—and changes of plan, like re-routing the ship—to fill everyone in at once. The crew would be waiting for that before the discussions *really* got started.

"Well," said Trove. "I ought to rouse Francis."

"Indeed. And I've got a ship to redirect."

"Thanks, Miss Brady."

"Don't mention it."

Trove got to his feet and wended back through the room. Natasha watched him go, then picked up her tray and headed for the doorway herself.

2

The command centre was empty when Natasha arrived. She was glad. Chitchat didn't feel to be her strong suit today.

She fell down into the seat at her usual console, cycled through to the navigation controls, inputted her passcodes and then set to work.

Last night she'd forked the ship almost ninety degrees off their original course; an hour later, she'd forked again, then followed a swaying, uneven curve for another two and a half hours. Since then the Pantheon had been travelling more or less in a straight line, not quite in the direction of *The Oft-Trodden Footpath*, but not too far off-course that they couldn't pick it back up.

She entered the co-ordinates on the slip Trove had given her, checked them twice, then told the computer to do its thing. A few moments later it drew up a refined flight path, pointing starboard. Wherever they were headed was eleven days' travel away, maybe faster if she spoke to Benjamin and got him to put the Volum through its paces. Which essentially meant overfeeding it to the nth degree, and praying a power spike didn't knock the Pantheon's systems offline. It was already bad enough with the one battery on the fritz.

Natasha gave the final okay to the computer, then waited. After five seconds, she felt it, just slightly; the minute tug that meant the Pantheon was changing direction.

"Morning."

Natasha glanced to the doorway. Ruby walked in. For the little sleep she'd had—probably none at all, Natasha thought—she looked remarkably perky.

"Morning, Captain." Natasha snapped a salute, but Ruby waved her off as she dropped down into a nearby chair.

"Trove gave you my instructions?"

"That he did; we're moving on our new course already."

"Excellent!" Ruby grinned. "He told you what we're searching for?"

"He did."

Ruby's grin extended, and she straightened in her seat, looking positively enthralled. "I think they were searching for it—the people on the Modicum. I found it in the captain's diary. Seems he went a little bit mad before ever finding it."

"And you don't think that the search is what *drove* him mad?" Natasha ventured. "It is, after all, a *ghost* armada."

Ruby shrugged. "Perhaps; I don't suppose there's any way we'll know. Regardless, we have one set of co-ordinates. We'll scope it out, and if it's a wild goose chase, well, it's a wild goose chase. Nothing ventured, nothing gained."

That was true. Natasha doubted they would find anything; this was a fable, or the ravings of a homicidal lunatic. Still, if it pleased Ruby, then she would go along with the ride. Especially now their pantry was full again.

Very suddenly, Ruby said, "You speak to Francis a lot."

"I do."

"How does he seem to you?"

Natasha's mouth quirked. "Perfectly fine. He's angry, and scared, but given the circumstances ..." She trailed off. "He's coped remarkably well."

"Hm." Ruby's lips tightened. She eyed the nearest screen—a schematic of the ship and a scrolling reel of status reports—but didn't seem to take it in.

"Something on your mind?"

"It's just ... strange." Ruby's words came slowly. "He doesn't appear to like me very much—and then a man appears from nowhere, trying—I assume, given the gun—to kill me. Escorted by Francis."

"A man who pointed that same gun at Francis's head," Natasha reminded her. When Ruby didn't reply, she continued, "I'm confident of his character."

"He hasn't been aboard long."

Natasha repeated, "I'm confident of his character."

There was a moment of quiet, but that seemed to seal it. Ruby nodded, then rose from her seat. "Okay. I'll see you later, Natasha." She crossed to the door. Just before she stepped over the threshold, she paused and looked back. "Just ... keep an eye on him, will you?"

Natasha nodded. "That I will."

Ruby smiled, and then was gone.

3

Just as the morning had come too fast for Natasha, it had also come too fast for Francis. He wasn't even sure if he'd slept; the entire night he'd tossed and turned, alternately going over everything Natasha had said, and fearing that every tiny sound from the ship was someone else dropping in unexpected.

Now he stared blearily at the ceiling. Sometime soon, Trove would knock, asking if he was ready for breakfast.

As if summoned by the thought alone, there were three raps against the door.

Francis climbed out of bed mechanically, crossed the room in his pyjamas, and opened the door. There was Trove, looking his usual self. Had he slept last night? Had *anyone* on this ship?

"Good morning," said Trove. "Breakfast is just being served."

"I think I'll skip it today," Francis said.

"Oh?"

"Yeah. Not feeling especially hungry."

"I see. I suppose it has been a rather exciting twenty-four hours." Trove shuffled his clipboard from beneath one arm to the other. "Very well. It'll be available for another thirty minutes if you change your mind. If not, I'll give you a knock around lunchtime."

"Thanks."

The door closed, and Francis fell onto the bed.

It had taken the full night's thought, but Francis had decided: maybe Natasha was right. Someone willing to send an assassin in the dead of night, who himself was perfectly happy to stick a gun to Francis's head—well, that person probably didn't have his best interests at heart.

… maybe. Because Francis couldn't shake that tiny niggle of doubt in the back of his mind. After all, he'd been referred to as 'stolen property'. And though, yes, a gun had been pressed into his temple, it was Ruby the assailant had been after. Francis just happened to be the person unlucky enough to have been stumbled upon.

Still, it didn't do to think about. That man was dead, and they'd fled at full speed. The chance of getting back to *The Pharmacologist's Eden* was a big fat zero.

So Francis needed another plan.

Ruby had told him there was no one around for hundreds of miles that had the capability to take him home. And maybe that was true, but they were due to pull into port any day now. Maybe Francis could poke around, ask some questions; see if he could be pointed in the right direction. Natasha might even be willing to help. She seemed to understand what he was going through, even if the captain herself didn't, with her ill-begotten ideas at integrating him into Pantheon life.

Yes, Francis decided. He would speak to Natasha and see what she said, and maybe, just maybe, he might be able to find an avenue home after all.

4

Ruby was sat in her study, leafing through the diary from the Modicum, when her communicator chimed. It was Evans; he was supposed to be midway through wiring up their new cameras.

"How can I help?" she said into the receiver.

"There's been a bit of a problem."

When she arrived at the bottom deck of the ship, Ruby said, "So I see."

Most of the Pantheon's machinery was clustered down here, including the two batteries that stored excess power from the Volum. Battery One had shorted out *again*, and in turn caused a fault in one of the condensers.

The Pantheon housed two water condensing units: one to the ship's front, another at the rear. They poked out into the atmosphere via apertures in the exterior panelling. Their job was simple: to condense water vapour, purify it, and store it for drinking water, as well as recycling as much waste possible.

It was the rear condenser they clustered around now. Its entire contents had flooded out, pooling half an inch deep.

"Can we fix it?" Ruby asked.

"I'd need to tinker with it," Evans said. "Couldn't say right now. It's amazing the batteries didn't get wet."

"Hm." Ruby glanced about. "We'll need to move the perishables out of harm's way." Peters nodded at this and wheeled into motion, flitting away. "And all of our weapons; gunpowder, cannonballs—is that safe?"

"Should be," said Mikhail. "It's all on racks."

"Would you check?"

"On it, Captain."

Ruby frowned as she considered the dead machine. One condenser could certainly generate enough water for the ship, and one battery was more than enough to keep it powered, along with the rest of the Pantheon. Still, it wasn't ideal; with one of each down, they were out of back-ups.

"See if you can get this thing fixed," Ruby said.

"What about the water?" Evans asked.

"Poke some holes so it can drain. Only small, mind, and make sure they're plugged once all is said and done. Any excess, the other condenser should absorb. Can you do that?"

"Aye."

"Good." Ruby gave the room another sweeping gaze, then headed along the short corridor. The door to the Volum room, and Benjamin, remained closed. "Has Benjamin been out at all?"

"Are you thinking of the same Ben I am?" Evans called back. "I doubt he's even noticed."

Ruby pulled a face. She knocked twice on the door and waited. After ten seconds and no reply, she knocked harder.

It jerked open. "*What*—" began an irate voice.

"Good morning," Ruby greeted. "You're looking well."

The irritation left Ben's face—though not necessarily because he was no longer irritated. "Morning, Captain." He patted at his messy hair, smoothing it to one side. "How can I assist?"

"This deck has been flooded. Had you noticed?"

"I—" Benjamin started. He looked down. To emphasise, Ruby lifted a boot. A momentary waterfall cascaded, ending in a trickle of raindrops. "I did."

"And you didn't think to investigate?"

Benjamin looked pained. "I was writing, Miss Celeste."

"I daresay you were." Ruby let her boot fall and peered past Benjamin into the Volum room. The floor glistened under the Volum's soft blue light. "Battery One failed and knocked out a condenser. Mikhail, Evans and Peters will need access to make some drainage holes in your floor." Before Ben could open his mouth very far, Ruby continued, "You like your privacy when studying, and I understand that. However, I won't allow the hull to become damaged in order to preserve that privacy for barely more than an hour. Do you understand?"

From the look on his face, Benjamin did understand, even if he did not agree, but he nodded and said, "Yes, Captain."

"Good." Ruby stepped forward to glance more fully into the room, causing Benjamin to inch back. Somewhat begrudgingly, given the expression that crossed his face.

He had been writing, of course he had; ledgers were spread over every surface, just like always. There was also a stack of plates, the topmost sporting a half-eaten piece of toast and semi-congealed streak of beans.

"I see you've been eating, even if you never come to the canteen," Ruby said.

"Sam brings me my meals."

"That's very kind of him. I daresay you would die of starvation if he didn't."

Benjamin let out a very small non-committal laugh.

"Well, I shan't keep you from your studies any longer," said Ruby. She receded through the door. "They'll be in soon, and will need to come back later to plug the holes back up. Do try not to give them a hard time."

"Yes, Captain."

"Perhaps you could spend some time elsewhere on the ship," she suggested half-seriously. "Pleasant though I'm sure your beard will become, you look rather more dashing when you've shaved."

Ben touched his face and the few days' worth of stubble that had accumulated, as if only just realising it had sprouted. Ruby *almost* laughed, but she held it in and turned away, listening to the door close behind her.

5

Francis wandered up the corridor. Ahead was the door to the ship's control room, and with it, Natasha. But her job must have been busier than he thought, because he'd come up and down this corridor at least a dozen times already, back and forth from the library to here to his quarters and over from the beginning again.

The door *was* closed, he'd told himself. There was obviously something going on in there, something keeping Natasha.

He could always knock. Just walk up and rap his fist on the door; done and over with in a couple of seconds. If Natasha was busy, fine; at least he'd know and wouldn't have to spend his morning stalking up and down the same part of the ship. But every time he got close, his determination left and he decided maybe he'd knock next time, or the time after that—or maybe he *could* wait, after all.

This time, though, he would do it.

He walked up to the door and stopped. Lifted a hand. Held it …

An alarm trilled, high and jarring, different to the one he'd heard before. Francis jerked and fell back against the wall. A second later the sound stopped, the door slid open, and out stepped Ruby, followed by Natasha. On seeing him, Ruby paused. An eyebrow lifted.

"Good morning, Francis," she said slowly. She glanced back and forth between him and Natasha. Licking her lip, she said, "I shall leave you to it," and then strode up the corridor.

"I'll assume you haven't been waiting outside and commend your good timing," Natasha said. She grinned, then nodded her head in the direction Ruby had gone. "Come on; Captain's called a meeting."

They fell into step.

"Where?"

"Cafeteria. Easiest place. And lunch is about to be served," she added with a check of the time on her communicator. "Two birds, one stone."

"Was that what the alarm was for?"

"You got it. There's no ship-wide intercom system set up; silly, if you ask me, but there we go." They turned a corner, trotting along behind Vala and Stefan, who were chattering up ahead. "How's your morning been?"

"Fine," Francis said. "I need to talk to you."

"Talk away, but make it quick."

"I was thinking," he started. "We're pulling into port sometime soon, right? Well, Ruby said there's no one around that has the capability to take me home, but that doesn't mean I can't ask around, right? Maybe someone will know a guy, or something. Maybe you could help."

Natasha's expression froze. Her jaw worked for a moment, and then she said, "Francis, I—"

They stepped into the cafeteria. Most of the crew were already in attendance; Benjamin was missing, as well as some of the technicians, who were presumably still in the ship's control centre. Everyone else had amassed against the rear wall. Ruby stood at the fore, beside Trove. She looked to Natasha and Francis as they came in.

"Aha, we're all here. Do find yourself a spot, Miss Brady."

Natasha and Francis took up position near the serving station. A troubled expression covered Natasha's face. She opened her mouth to whisper something to Francis's curious frown, but was cut off.

"Hello, everyone; it's been a while since I called us all together, so felt it pertinent we check in," said Ruby. "Especially following the past day or two's events.

"As you are all no doubt aware, yesterday morning we were fired upon by a passing ship."

"Hard to miss the impact vibrations," Mikhail said, to a round of snickers.

A smile worked at the corners of Ruby's lips. "Quite. We boarded and found it somewhat ... dilapidated, shall we say. Only the captain remained." The words hung in the air a moment, and Francis was sure Ruby didn't need to tell everyone what had happened to him. Sure enough, she continued by saying, "The Modicum's stores were almost full; as such, *our* stores are now almost full.

"We also salvaged this," Ruby said. She extended a hand to Trove, who handed her a leather-bound book. Francis peered, then glanced sideways at Natasha. She pulled a face, something he couldn't quite read, before averting her gaze.

"This diary belonged to the Modicum's captain. For the most part it's uninteresting, but at the end ..." Ruby flicked through to the final page. "A pair of co-ordinates. And the words 'Ghost Armada'."

She flipped the book closed and handed it back.

"Trove assures me the words are nothing more than the ravings of a deluded man in the grip of insanity. And I'm sure many of you will agree." A grin erupted on Ruby's face, an infectious smile that Francis saw spread to a good number of the crew—except for Natasha. "However, given the state of our stores, I've decided investigation is in order. On the off-chance, no matter how small, that there *is* something out there.

"As of this morning, the Pantheon has been re-routed. We will no longer be checking in at *The Oft-Trodden Footpath*, as planned, but will instead head directly for the purported location of this Ghost Armada."

Chatter sprung up all around him, but Francis didn't hear. His heart seemed to freeze in his chest. His blood ran cold. The world tunnelled.

The ship had been redirected. They weren't heading to the SkyPort.

And Francis wouldn't be able to ask anyone for a way home.

Dimly he was aware that someone had taken his wrist, squeezed it. Natasha.

"That's what you were doing in there," he muttered. "The control room, all morning."

Natasha nodded. "I changed the ship's direction first thing; since then we've been plotting course refinements, and Miss Celeste was briefing the techies, as they can't be here."

Francis stared blankly. All this morning he'd been waiting to speak with her, trekking up and down the hallway and staring at a closed door, unaware that on the other side his latest opportunity had already been snatched away from him.

"I'm sorry," Natasha said.

Above the hubbub, Ruby called, "That's enough conversation for now. I've answered all I can. In the meantime, there are a couple of other things I need to go through before we dismiss for lunch.

"Battery One failed earlier this morning and caused a fault in one of our condensers. It's getting fixed, but it sprung a leak all over the bottom deck. Take care if you're going down, because there are going to be a number of holes in the hull for the rest of the day.

"Oh, and yes," she added offhandedly, "we were boarded last night."

Another squall of noise went up. Ruby waved it down. "None of us knows anything; cameras didn't pick anything up, thus far we've discovered no identification upon him, and he was taken care of before we could extract any meaningful information. The main thing is that we're safe now. Regardless, be alert." She looked slowly around the room at each crew member's face as she spoke, seeming to linger just a moment longer on Francis. "Now; dismissed. Enjoy lunch."

A small cheer went up as everyone set into motion, heading for the serving station, and Francis and Natasha were bustled to one side.

"Do you want to talk about it?" Natasha said. "We could go somewhere private; library, maybe."

Somehow, a hollow laugh escaped Francis's lips. "What's there to talk about?"

"The ship changing direction. Getting home. Your *feelings*." But Francis simply stood mutely, stare lost somewhere within the floor. "Do you want to get some lunch?" Natasha offered lamely at last.

"No. Thanks."

"Are you sure?"

"Yeah. I think I'll just … head back to my room." He blinked, looked up at her for the first time in what seemed like hours. Natasha had expected there to be sadness wrought on his face, but there was nothing: he was blank. "See you later."

Away Francis shuffled, Natasha staring behind him, suddenly feeling much less hungry herself, too.

6

Lunch was a choice between sandwiches or soup, which was a shame, because that meant tomorrow's lunch would be leftover soup. Still, it made a pleasant change of pace from the days before encountering the Modicum.

Ruby wondered about that ship now, as she ate. The captain was dead, and no one else was on-board. It had been left drifting, an empty husk. How long would the Modicum's Volum last before it starved to death and the ship crashed onto the surface?

Perhaps that was something she would ask Benjamin. He would know.

The thought of the surface brought Francis back into her mind—not that he'd particularly left it. Why had he been hovering outside the control room?

Ruby glanced toward the corner table. Natasha sat alone. Nothing new there. But there was something off about her; some vacant, faraway look to her face. And she'd been talking about something in hushed tones with Francis before sitting down to eat, pressed into the corner of the room together. Something that had caused Francis to wander away—skipping yet another meal in favour of what?—and Natasha to look ... upset? What was she upset about?

"You look thoughtful, Miss Celeste," said Trove.

Ruby placed the last corner of her sandwich into her mouth and chewed slowly. Once she'd swallowed, she said, "I suppose I am." Turning her stare away from Natasha, she brushed the crumbs from her fingertips and picked up the diary, leafing through its pages. "Things have been somewhat eventful, wouldn't you say?"

"Somewhat," Trove agreed. He opened his mouth to say something, but his gaze shifted. "Good afternoon, Miss Brady."

Ruby looked around. Natasha had abandoned her table and now stood beside her captain, fingers laced behind her back.

"Trove," Natasha said with a nod. To Ruby she directed, "I wondered if I might speak with you in private."

"Absolutely. Trove, I shall be with you in a moment." Ruby rose, and she and Natasha exited the cafeteria and began to walk up the corridor. "Did you enjoy lunch?" she asked.

"A pleasant change, albeit somewhat bland," Natasha said.

"Hah. Quite."

They continued in silence for a few moments. When Natasha was confident the halls were empty, she said in a low voice, "I wondered if you might reconsider our trip."

"Oh?"

"Francis wants to stop off at a port so he can ask around, see if maybe there's someone who might be able to get him a ride home."

Ruby stopped walking; Natasha halted beside her. Frown lines creasing her forehead, Ruby removed her tricorne and smoothed her mass of crimson hair. "All the ports around here are small, pokey little places—he's not going to find someone. You know that just as well as I do."

"I know." Exasperation crept into Natasha's voice. "I do, but he's so desperate. Besides, it's something to focus on, and he could do with a ray of hope right now. All we'd need to do is pick up our old course; a couple days of extra travel, that's it. We've got the stores to handle it."

Ruby considered. Her fingers fretted at the folds of her hat. A twitch of her eyebrow, her lower lip; then she replaced the tricorne on her head, readjusted it, inhaled—and said, "No."

Natasha stared. "What?"

"No. Look, I understand what you're saying. But he's not going to find anyone; not here, not within a few hundred miles, probably not within a few *thousand*. Besides, they'll want payment, and we don't have enough to cover the jumped-up prices those sorts of people will be asking.

"Beyond that, we were *boarded* last night, lest you forget. It's imperative we get out of the area; it's a matter of safety.

"For now we're searching for the Ghost Armada. *Then* we can check into port and Francis can ask around. Otherwise, he's just going to have to wait. Whether we go now or later, the result is the same. He's stuck here."

Tension hung in the air, thick and palpable. Natasha stared at her captain, and for a long, drawn-out moment, Ruby thought she would say something to challenge her, or her face would betray the anger she was sure she could feel pulsing beneath the navigation leader's veins. But as the seconds ticked by nothing happened, and finally Natasha gave a very curt nod and said, "Very well." Snapping a salute, she turned back the way they'd come and marched away.

7

It was not unheard of for Ruby to stand over a body as the Pantheon's resident doctor sewed it back up, but the occurrence was rare. Fortunately, on this occasion it wasn't one of her crew in the process of being restitched.

"There was nothing at all?"

"Not a thing," said Darrel. He spoke from behind a bloody mouth guard. Blood also smeared his coveralls in browning patches. "Not that I expected to find anything, having said that. It was just nice to be able to keep in practise."

"I thought perhaps there might be something on him. *In* him," Ruby said, more to herself than Darrel.

"Ah yes, there might have been. And better safe than sorry." Darrel bent forward, pulled the final stitch tight, and cut the thread. "There. All finished."

Ruby pondered as the doctor set about removing his coveralls. Nothing in the man's clothes, no embedded identichips. Completely anonymous. Which meant he could have come from anywhere—though if what Natasha had passed on from Francis about having been referred to as 'stolen property' was true, it was likely he'd come from *The Pharmacologist's Eden*.

If.

"What shall we do with him?" Darrel asked, snapping Ruby from her thoughts.

"Dump him overboard. Little worth in keeping him. He's just ... meat," she said with distaste, waving a hand at the corpse.

"I'll bag him up." As Darrel pulled on a new pair of latex gloves, then a single body bag from a pull-out drawer beneath the bed the autopsy had been performed on, he said, "Will you be sending one of Mikhail's lads to do it?"

Ruby shook her head. "I'll take him."

"Ah."

"It was me he was after; seems fitting, wouldn't you say?"

"Hah, well, I suppose so, in that case."

Darrel opened the body bag and laid it upside-down over the corpse. Ruby sidestepped him, pulled on a pair of gloves of her own, and helped as they manoeuvred the bag around the dead man's extremities. Finally they flipped it over, the man nestled safely inside, and zipped it up.

"Thanks, Darrel," Ruby said. Carefully she pulled off her gloves, and threw them into the trash.

"Not a problem. Like I said, good to keep in practise."

Hefting the body over her shoulder, Ruby left the medical bay. This man had been lithe; trained with a gun, not swords and heavy lifting. Despite that, he wasn't as light as she'd expected—or maybe her lack of sleep was finally gaining on her.

Trove waited outside. He gave the body bag an unpleasant look, then fell into step beside Ruby.

"Any luck?" he asked.

"No, unfortunately. Still, doesn't matter; Natasha took us off in the middle of the night, so we're safe. And now we've changed direction entirely, this man's buddies aren't going to find us."

"You're dumping the body?"

"Perhaps," said Ruby. "I wondered if maybe Samuel might like it if I added it to the pantry. Give us something a little bit different to eat." She glanced sideways at Trove's paled face, and laughed. "Yes, I'm dumping it."

"I see. I expect I'll regret asking this, but how do you plan on getting it through the porthole by yourself? Mikhail usually has one of the others help him."

Ruby pulled her most dazzling smile. "Well, Trove, seeing as you're here perhaps you can assist me."

He sighed. "I thought you'd say that."

Extricating the body through the porthole wasn't too difficult, though Ruby did think Trove might lose his lunch as he manhandled it up into her waiting arms.

"On our next ship," he panted, clutching the rungs of the ladder once the task was complete, "we should have a regular door onto the deck, instead of a hole you can only get through by ladder."

Ruby tutted. "What do you mean, next ship? Do you expect me to crash this one?"

"Expect, no. But hope, after that …"

Smirking, Ruby dismissed him. "Have a sit-down; I'll meet up with you again later."

"For more pleasant jobs like this one? I look forward to it."

Ruby hefted the body back onto her shoulder and wandered up the deck, heading for the ship's rear. At the back railing, she stopped, then tossed the bag forward in as unceremonious a fashion she could muster. Leaning over the edge, she watched the black shape tumble until it was a smear, then a dot, and then gone.

"I don't envy the person that finds that," she muttered, before heading back up the deck.

8

At dinnertime, there was a knock at Francis's door. He'd been lying in bed, and with nary a glance at the entryway, he hustled further beneath the covers. Trove could wait, for all he cared; Francis wasn't coming out. Not tonight, and maybe not tomorrow either.

The knock came again. A long pause followed. When Francis counted to a minute, he thought, *Good, he's gone.*

Then a third knock. And a voice:

"Francis, open up. I know you're in there."

Natasha?

Sitting upright and throwing the covers off, he crossed the room in three strides and tugged the door open. Just beyond, hand hovering and ready to knock again, was Natasha. She paused, stared at Francis, and let her hand drop.

"Hi."

Francis: "Hi."

"I thought I'd check on you."

"Oh."

Francis waited lamely. On the other side of the door frame, Natasha did the same.

She sighed. "Can I come in? Or would you like to go somewhere?"

Francis hesitated, then stepped aside. "Come in." Natasha

passed him, and he closed the door. "Sorry about the mess." He gestured at the bed and its tangle of covers. "I was lying down."

"That's okay." Natasha pulled out the chair by the desk. "Mind if I sit here?"

"Go ahead."

She sat. Francis stood idle for a moment, then realised he ought to do the same. Smoothing the covers, he made the bed as presentable as he could be bothered—which wasn't very, but anything was better than the unkempt pit it had been—and lowered himself on it. He shuffled up to the wall and pulled his knees into his chest, and waited.

"My quarters are about the same," Natasha said. Aha: pointless chitchat. "They all are on the ship; minor layout changes, but …"

She trailed off. Her eyes roved the room. When they finally landed on Francis, he lifted his head from where he'd been leaning on his arms and said, "What are you here for?"

"I said; to check on you. You were upset earlier."

A hollow laugh escaped him. "Of course I was."

"So I wondered if maybe you wanted to talk about it."

"Talk about what? About the fact I'm stuck here? About the fact I don't have a ride home, and the only avenue I could think of has been snatched away because this ship's lunatic captain wants to search for *ghosts*? What am I supposed to say?"

"It's not ideal, I know."

"Not ideal?" Francis exploded. Suddenly he was on his feet, arms gesticulating wildly. "I was *kidnapped*, Natasha, and now I'm stuck here with no way back! My parents, my whole life—all of that was ripped away from me, and the one possible way I could get back, the one tiny shred of hope I've had, was crushed this morning when Ruby-poxy-Celeste decided she wanted to go after a horde of fucking *ghost ships*! What am I supposed to say about any of that?"

Natasha, calmly: "You're supposed to talk about your feelings."

"How do you *think* I'm feeling?" Francis roared. "Look at me! Listen to me! Am I shouting?"

"Yes."

"So how do you think I feel?"

"Angry?"

"Yes! Of course I'm angry!"

"And scared?"

"Scared? Let me think," Francis said, tapping his chin in mock thought. "I'm trapped floating in the sky, on a ship captained by someone who I've seen murder *several times now*—oh, and last night someone descended from the sky in the middle of the night and pointed a *gun* at my head. Yes, Natasha, I'm scared." Now he softened, the tension leaving his body; slumping, he let out a long, defeated sigh. "I'm terrified. And … and … and I just shouted at about the only friend I've got on this ship. Because she was looking out for me."

Dropping onto the bed, Francis shuffled back against the wall and wrapped his legs in his arms again. His head drooped against his forearms. Hiding.

Lowly, he said, "I'm sorry. I shouldn't have done that."

"That's okay." Natasha's voice was soft. She moved from the chair to the bed and laid a hand against Francis's wrist. Light, but enough to feel reassuring. "You needed to get it out.

"You know," she carried on after a pause, "I tried to get Ruby to change direction; just to pull us into port."

Francis looked up. "You did?"

"Yes. She declined."

Oh. Well, wasn't that a surprise.

"Just as you said, we were boarded last night," Natasha said carefully. "We were heading to *The Oft-Trodden Footpath* on a straight vector, and the person that boarded us was looking for Ruby specifically. Just in case anyone else is out there, the change of course is for the best. I mean, you wouldn't want to get snatched by someone even worse than Stein while you're asking around, would you?"

Francis didn't reply. He wanted to find some argument, something that would let him rail against Ruby's reasons, but nothing came to mind. Natasha was right, again.

"We'll still check into port," Natasha said. "It'll be a couple of weeks out, but you can still ask around. And I'll help you."

Then she hesitated. Francis sat up straight, wariness seeping in. "But?" he prompted.

"There's something you should know." Natasha's words came slowly, and it took everything Francis had in him not to press her to speak faster. "What you were told before, about there being no one in this area with the capability to get down to the surface— well, it's true. But it's a little more far-reaching than that. People that have the tech to get to the surface and back again—they're very few and far between. I've been on this ship for four years, travelled all over, and Rhod Stein was one of only a handful I've heard of that could do it."

"But," Francis started. "But—but if he can, someone else could?"

"I don't know who, or how," Natasha said. "The Volum can keep us aloft here, but closer to the ground ... Volum, and ships, are designed to stay in the air. If they drop too close to the surface—"

"They're too heavy to lift again," Francis finished. "But somehow Rhod had a way; he had to. So maybe someone else does too."

Natasha nodded. "I imagine some do, here and there. But it's very, very costly."

"It can't have been too costly for Rhod. Otherwise he wouldn't have snatched me. He wanted to sell me, right? He had to have been making a profit. And if I was cheap enough for Ruby to buy, and Rhod was making a profit—surely she can cover the price. Right?"

"No." Natasha sighed and rearranged herself on the edge of the bed. "Your cost—it was paid in instalments. One fee upfront, and then monthly payments for the next fifteen years; like a mortgage. If it was a single cost, Ruby would never have been able to purchase you."

Quiet. Then: "So what you're saying is I *am* stuck here."

"No. We're going to ask around as soon as we pull into the next port, I promise." Natasha reached out again and touched his wrist. "But I want to be realistic with you. There is hope—but it may not be much."

The room fell into silence. Not even Francis's mind was working: it had stalled, fallen still. No ceaseless examination of everything he'd just been told, no turning it over in every direction, desperately hoping to spot some small hole through which he might root out an escape. Only a death knell rang in his mind.

"I'm sorry," said Natasha.

Francis shrugged. "Not your fault. Thanks for being honest with me."

"I'm sorry I didn't do it sooner."

"You were looking out for me."

"Do you want to talk about it?"

"No," Francis said with a tiny shake of the head. "I … I think I'd like to be alone now."

"Okay. But if you change your mind, find me."

"Will do."

The door swung open, then shut. Francis didn't look up as Natasha left.

For a long time, he sat and stared, listening to the noises of the ship, feeling the subtle pull as a course refinement nudged the Pantheon along a slightly different vector. No thought went through his brain; just Natasha's words, stark and clear. Defeat had piled upon him, and this time the miniscule opportunity to snatch victory from its jaws was so quantum as to not even exist.

Sighing, he lay down on the bed and stared at the ceiling. At some point, the bulb above him flickered for an instant. It would flicker again, for longer, but by that time Francis had been defeated for the second time today: by sleep.

Integration

(Chapter Nine)

1

The mood Francis woke up in the following morning was complex, but heralded by one single word as he stared at the ceiling:

Home.

This was it. Here, the Pantheon, was his home now. These people were his new family. And that meant acting like it. No sitting around in libraries with books, hoping to avoid everyone (or almost everyone); no more shutting himself in this room with nothing to do but sit idly and think over the same thing again and again. No more being closed off, no more acting little more than a prisoner with privileges. Yes, he was stuck, but that didn't mean he had to be sullen for the rest of his life, even if it was a life aboard a flying ship.

It was a strange series of emotions: part resignation, part defeat, but also part determination, too.

This processed, Francis climbed out of bed. He pulled on his clothes; a blue shirt that didn't fit, and trousers that were almost tight enough at his waist but far too wide at his heels. Surveying himself in the mirror, he pulled at the loose folds of material. What was it Ruby had said, back on his first morning here? That was it: Vala was the ship's seamstress; she could take the clothes in. Maybe he would catch her at breakfast.

Instead of waiting for Trove, he left his room and wandered down the corridor to the cafeteria. No one else was there, and in fact Samuel was still filling the serving station. Today there was omelette and toast, or cereal.

"Morning," Francis said.

Samuel grunted and waved a hand; not ready yet.

Francis hovered outside for a few minutes, wondering if anyone else would arrive soon. Then Samuel grunted something again, which Francis took to mean, "You can come in now," and so he stepped back through the door, grabbed a tray, plate and cutlery, and let Samuel drop an omelette and two slices of buttered toast down for him.

"Thanks."

Another grunt.

With pick of the tables, he perched down alongside a wall. He eyed the position Natasha usually took, over in the corner; perhaps he could sit with her when she arrived. Or maybe wave her over.

He'd start by apologising for last night, he thought. Then maybe he'd ask what he could do aboard the ship to help out. Probably nothing in the control centre; all those workstations had looked rather technical. But maybe she could give him some advice, or even training.

Two-thirds of Francis's omelette was gone by the time the trickle of diners got started. It hadn't taken long; he was famished after another day of pointlessly starving himself. Probably he'd be completely finished before Natasha even arrived.

"Morning," said Herschel as he passed; Francis, mid-chew, swallowed hard and choked out a response.

Amelie next; then Evans and Peters, already laughing about something; then Vala and Stefan. Francis watched as they were served together, Vala opting for cereal and Stefan taking an extra slice of toast when Samuel's back was turned. As they headed toward their usual spot, Francis put down his knife and fork and waved a hand.

"Vala—hey."

Confusion swept her face for a second—this was the first time Francis had ever spoken to her, after all—before she smiled, patted

Stefan on the arm and then crossed to Francis.

"Good morning," she said. "What can I do for you?"

"Um, Ruby said you're the ship's seamstress?"

"That I am."

"Would you be able to take my clothes in for me?" Grabbing a fold of his too-large shirt, Francis flapped it. "Most of them are kind of big."

"Of course! Do you know your measurements?"

"Um, no." Francis's cheeks coloured. "Sorry."

"Not a worry. I've got measuring tape; we'll get you sorted."

"Excellent. Thanks."

"Are you free today?" Vala asked. "I've got a couple of hours after breakfast. It's short-notice, but Stefan's got the afternoon off. And I rather think I ought to spend it with him, given he's my husband," she added in a lower voice, winking conspiratorially.

"Yeah, of course," said Francis.

"You know where my room is?"

"I think so."

"Well, it has my name on it, so just check out the plaque." Smiling again, Vala glanced at her bowl. "I'd better get to the table, or these are going to go soggy."

"Oh, yeah, sorry."

"See you shortly, Francis."

And off she went.

Francis had barely chewed half of his bite of toast before there was a small noise of surprise. Looking around, he saw Trove wending his way toward him.

"You're already here," he observed. "I've just been knocking at your door."

"I woke up early," Francis said with a shrug. "Thought I may as well come down, see what was on the menu."

"Something unpleasant, I've come to expect."

"Omelette and toast. Not bad."

"I daresay you'll reconsider after you've been here longer." Trove paused. "Well, I shall get breakfast of my own, then."

He trotted away and joined the small queue. Francis eyed them, but Natasha wasn't among the tiny throng: Darrel was making conversation with Mikhail, and beside them was a waiflike woman who Francis had seen only once or twice: one of the night-shift technicians, apparently joining Stefan's ranks in having a day to herself.

A minute or so later, Trove rejoined Francis at the table with an omelette and toast of his own. Wordlessly, he pushed the toast onto Francis's empty plate, before cutting off a small piece of omelette.

"Um," said Francis.

"Thought you could do with the sustenance after yesterday's hunger strike." Trove ate a small square of egg, then pulled a face. "Besides, Samuel's cooking rarely agrees with me. Even the toast."

"I see. Err, thanks."

2

There was still no sign of Natasha by the time Vala had finished her cereal, so she and Francis left together.

Vala and Stefan had a larger room than Francis's, longer by around two-thirds. Instead of a single there was a double bed—which turned out to be two singles pushed together. The decoration was far less sparse, too; embroidery was mounted in several places, books were arranged neatly on shelves, on the desk was an enormous fold-out box of Vala's sewing equipment—needles, thread, boxes of thimbles of all different sizes, off-cuts of materials—and beside it was a mannequin adorned by a half-finished chemise, blue material flowing halfway to the floor. But most noticeable were the hordes of plants packing the space, from spidery little things to a miniature tree with waxy red leaves. One of the smaller plants was flowering, heads fat and purple.

"That's a *charis*," Vala said. "I expect you have them down on the surface, don't you?"

"Maybe," said Francis. "I don't know much about plants." He stepped closer and bent down. A subtle tang wafted up at him. Under the lights, tiny specks in the petals sparkled. "It looks like glitter."

"That's why I like it." Vala gave the plant an affectionate look, then set about foraging in her sewing box. "Stefan got it for me; wedding present."

"Have you been married long?"

"Two years, eight months." Vala pulled out a plastic box of needles and laid them aside. "And sixteen days, but don't tell him I'm counting.

"Now, if you drop that pile of clothes on the bed there—that'll do, thanks—we can get started. If you can stand just here ..." Vala waved Francis into the small amount of free space in the middle of the floor. "Perfect. Now, hold your arms up—little bit higher—here we go, like that. Hold still."

She began to fuss over him, starting with the shirt, wadding up material and then beginning to pin back folds. Francis twitched at the first feel of cold metal.

"I shan't stab you; these are practised hands," Vala said.

The shirt done with, she moved down to his trousers.

"Let me just move this leg," she said, pulling at his ankle. Francis obliged, and Vala's folding and pinning resumed.

"You should have come to see me sooner. I could have got these tightened up for you in no time."

"Sorry. I guess I was distracted."

"Yes, you did have that air about you. I must say, you rather surprised me this morning. It may well have been the first time I've heard you speak."

"Sorry," Francis said again.

"Don't worry! Nothing to apologise for."

Once both of the legs were filled with pins, Vala returned to her sewing box. She produced a measuring tape and a small pad, upon which was clipped a tiny pencil. Flicking through pages of delicate numbers, she found a blank spot close to the back and smoothed the book open.

"I'm just going to measure you so we don't have to pin all of these," she said. "Arms up again—there we are, that's it."

She hummed to herself as she moved around Francis, wrapping the tape about him in every place she could seem to think of, then noting down what it read. Now or again she would scrutinise the folds she'd pinned back, mutter something to herself and revise a figure, then carry on.

"So what's it like down there?" she asked after a while.

"Hm?"

"The surface."

"Oh. Um." Francis thought. He wanted to shrug, but didn't dare risk moving for all the needles. "It's nice. I live in a little town. There's a park near me, with a pond. Some fields; agriculture. Just … normal, I suppose."

"I've seen pictures," Vala said. "Of cities and things, and nature. I find it rather interesting."

"You're the first person to ask me about it."

"Am I? I'd have thought Miss Brady …" She trailed off. "We're all curious, Francis. But you've … well, had some trouble adjusting, so we've been letting you get your head around things."

"I see."

"Can your people get up here?" Vala asked.

Now Francis did shrug, just slightly; the tiniest incline he could give to his shoulders without really shifting. "Maybe. I don't know." He pondered. Sadness crept into his stomach, so he shifted the conversation. "Do you have towns and cities up here? Or does everyone just fly around in ships?"

"We do indeed have towns and cities," Vala said. "And forests, too."

Francis frowned. "What?"

"Floating islands. They're rather rare, but a glorious sight."

"But how—"

"Packed full of Volum, I imagine." Vala took one last measurement about Francis's heel, noted it, and made a satisfied noise. "All done. I can get to work on the rest of these." She started pulling pins out again, dropping them into their container, which lay open next to Francis's feet.

"Will they take long?"

"Not very. I won't get much done today, because of Stefan's day off." She gave an exaggerated roll of the eyes and a mock tut. Francis smiled. "But tomorrow I'll get most of the way through; maybe even the lot. You're okay for clothes today and tomorrow, aren't you?"

Francis nodded. "Got the clothes I came here in for tomorrow, and these for today."

"Yes—drop these ones in to me tomorrow morning after breakfast, will you? And hopefully in a couple of days' time you'll have the equivalent of a whole new wardrobe to kit yourself out in."

Francis grinned at that. "Thank you."

"Not a problem. Have a good day, Francis."

"You too."

Vala was already starting when Francis left the room, sat down at her table and withdrawing spools of thread to match the topmost shirt on Francis's stack. He pulled the door closed, then fiddled with all the spare material flapping around his midriff. Perhaps he ought to have kept those pins in place after all.

3

The door to the Pantheon's control centre was open as Francis passed by. He glanced inside; Amelie was already at a console, scrolling through green text, as was Stefan further back. There was also Natasha, balancing a plate precariously on her knee and eating toast.

"Hi," Francis said from the doorway.

She looked up and waved him in. "Morning."

"This your breakfast?" Francis asked.

"Yes," Natasha answered, long and low. "I woke up late; poor sleep," she confided. Brushing crumbs from her fingers onto the plate, she rearranged herself in the chair and said, "So what can I do for you?"

"I was wondering if maybe there might be a job you could give me. Something to do."

"Oh?" One of Natasha's eyebrows quirked. "Well, I don't really know. There's not a lot I can give to you in here; it's pretty specialist, and the hours are long."

"Hear, hear," Stefan called from the back of the room.

"Why don't you go find Mikhail?" Natasha suggested. "He does a lot of general work; much more varied and interesting than staring at numbers and diagnostic reports."

"Okay. Do you know where I can find him?"

"They're on the bottom deck today. Plugging the holes they made in the floor." Natasha cast a distracted glance at her screen, then back to Francis. "Sorry I can't help more. Is that okay, talking to Mikhail?"

"Sure, fine. Thanks."

"Any time."

"Are you free this evening?" Francis asked.

"Should be. Anything in mind?"

He shrugged. "Hang out."

"Good enough plan. I'll catch you later."

Francis wandered from the control room and headed for the stairs between levels.

Now, mid-morning looming, most people on the ship were awake. As he passed the cafeteria, he spotted Herschel cleaning up—relegated to janitorial duty, apparently. Beyond the serving station, Francis could see Samuel bent over the ship's huge oven, stirring a pan.

Voices sung up from the bottom deck before Francis was even partway down the stairs. No wonder: Evans and Peters were hollering songs back and forth as they each perched over a fist-sized hole in the floor, filling the gaps with a thick, sludgy grey substance. Further back, squatted over a hole of his own, was

Mikhail, whose face was creased with sniggers.

"Morning," Francis called nervously.

Three faces looked up. The singing ceased. Peters cast a momentary look at Evans and then Mikhail, then gave Francis a nod. "Morning, Francis."

"I wondered if maybe there was a job," Francis said.

"Aha." Mikhail that time. "You did?" He stood. A rag was stuffed into his belt; pulling it out, he wiped his hands, then stepped forward and joined Francis. He stuck out his hand, and they shook. "Anything in mind?"

Francis shrugged. "Natasha said you'd be able to suggest something."

"Smart woman, that Natasha," said Mikhail. "Well, right now we're doing exactly what you see: sealing holes. It's not interesting work, but it's simple enough to get started on. Sound good?"

Francis nodded. "Sure."

"Good stuff. Come on over, I'll walk you through it."

"Keep half an eye on us," Evans said to Francis as they walked past him. "He's a liability. Might teach you wrong and only realise in a day's time, when there's a bloody great hole in the bottom of the ship."

"Or worse," Peters added.

"Comedians," said Mikhail. To Francis: "You've met these two clowns, right? Reuben Evans, and Glim Peters." He pointed at each in turn, and the two men pulled cheesy grins. Peters even crossed his eyes. "What names, eh?"

"Says *Mikhail*," Peters called. "Who names their kid *Mikhail*?"

"Ignore him," Mikhail said to Francis. "He's still sore his parents misspelled their feelings at having bore him as a child."

"What's that then?"

"*Glum.*"

Evans guffawed; Peters scooped up a handful of the grey goop and flicked it at him, painting a dirty line across his overalls. Evans shouted, "Hey!" and Peters shot him a dark grin, before going back to shouting the song he'd been crooning before Francis descended the stairs.

"Like children," Mikhail said, shaking his head with a smile. "They're hoping to piss off Benjamin," he told Francis.

Francis glanced at the door to the Volum room. Closed. "Has he been out at all?"

"Not yet. Only a matter of time, though; those two have been getting louder."

Squatting down again beside the hole he'd been filling, Mikhail patted the deck. Francis sunk to a crouch, half-trying not to stare out of the hole. Wisps of cloud were just visible, and beyond was a patch of green blurred by the cover of cotton.

"This here is sealant," Mikhail said. He lifted up a plastic tub which was filled with grey goo. Placing the tub back down, he lifted a smaller container: this one round and filled with black powder, as well as a plastic scoop. "In the presence of this, it's quick-drying, which is always handy. It's as strong as steel, which is why we're using it to patch up these holes.

"The trick is to mix them and act fast. You've got about ten seconds before it starts to rubberise, and then thirty seconds after that it's solid as a rock."

Next to Mikhail's knees was a flat-headed tool and something that looked as though it might once have been a plate, before becoming a stained, uneven mess. Taking the tool in hand, Mikhail said, "It's relatively easy once you get into a rhythm. First, a spot of this." With his free hand, he poured out a generous amount of goo. It gave off a plasticky odour, and Francis pulled a face. "Pleasant, isn't it?"

"Can't be worse than you," Evans called over. Mikhail stuck up his middle finger.

"Now a spoon of this." He scooped out a pile of black powder. "And now we mix."

With quick, assured movements, he used the scraper to churn goo and powder together. The smell intensified for a second, and then was abruptly replaced by what Francis could only describe as burning. His nose scrunched up.

"That's the smell you're waiting for," said Mikhail. "Soon as you smell that, you're set to plug the hole."

To demonstrate, he scooped up the material. It came all as one gelatinous lump. With a flip, he pushed it down over the hole. Though Francis thought it might simply fall through, it did no such thing: when Mikhail lifted the scraper and began to smooth over the top, it held firm. After a few more movements that looked too casual to be as precise as they surely were, it was almost impossible to see where the hull and sealant joined.

"Done." Mikhail sat back and looked across to Francis. "Think you can manage that?"

"I might need to watch it again first," Francis said.

Mikhail laughed. "Not a problem, not a problem. Plenty of holes down here; we had a lot of water to drain."

"Yeah." Francis looked about. Mikhail was right: there were pocks everywhere. "What actually happened?"

"Battery malfunction caused a fault in one of our water condensers," Evans said. "Spilled its contents everywhere."

"Techie here is meant to be repairing it," Peters chimed, pointing at Evans with his scoop. "Hasn't managed yet though. Reckon he's lost his knack, I do. Might have to get a *real* techie in here to fix it."

Evans responded with a string of expletives, and then affixed Paige with a grin. "Glum doesn't know what he's talking about. Difficult things, those condensers. It'll be up and running again in no time. Which is more than I can say for him if he's not careful."

"Oh yeah? What're you going to do?"

"Shove this where the sun doesn't shine, then plug the gap with sealant so you never—"

"Let's leave them to it," Mikhail said. Shuffling over to the next hole, he said, "Come on, I'll do this one, then you can try the next."

It turned out plugging holes *was* more difficult than Mikhail made it look. Francis's first attempt dried before the hole was filled, and the second time he didn't pour out quite enough, so instead of holding firm it simply dropped through the gap.

"Ouch," Mikhail said as he watched it disappear. "Someone's going to feel that."

The third attempt went slightly better though, and every one after that followed the same pattern of gradual improvement. Although they didn't look quite as smooth as Mikhail's, with their uneven joins and smeary tops, Francis was pleased with his handiwork.

The morning vanished before Francis's eyes. It felt like he'd only been at work for less than an hour when Mikhail checked the time on his communicator and clapped his hands together.

"Lunch time, lads. We'll get back to this shortly."

"That's a shame," said Peters. "I was really enjoying Reuben's singing."

"Yeah," Evans said. "It's a shame Ben seems to be enjoying it too. Look: hasn't even cracked the door to tell me to stop. I feel like a failure."

4

"Whatcha reading?"

Francis looked up. In the doorway to the library stood Natasha, arm leaned casually against the frame, crooked smile on her face.

"Some story," Francis said. He flipped the book closed and lifted it to show Natasha the cover. "Don't know what it's called; name has faded."

"Any good?"

"Not really." Francis placed it aside. "So what are we doing?"

"Sit and read?" Natasha suggested. Francis pulled a face, and she said, "Unless you have any other ideas?"

"I wondered," Francis said, and hesitated. "Maybe we could go sit on the top deck."

"Aha. Sightseeing?"

"Something like that."

They headed up. Francis worried he might chicken out when he reached the ladder, and for a second a flashback of his last excursion topside—every excursion, really—played in his mind. But he overcame it and climbed, feet slow and careful on the rungs, finally pulling himself through the porthole and trying his hardest not to look at the edges.

"Still afraid, huh?" Natasha asked.

"Got to face it sometime," he muttered.

"Hah. Come on, we'll do it together."

She looped her arm around his and stepped in close. "You ready?" Francis nodded, and Natasha laughed. "You don't look ready. You look decidedly pale."

"Let's just be slow about this," he said.

Along the deck they walked, arms linked. When Francis paused, Natasha paused too, waiting patiently until he was ready to carry on. When he took a step, no matter how small or hesitant, she matched it, not stepping further ahead nor lagging behind. She chattered to him about her day, engaging him just enough to keep his mind from focussing entirely on this short jaunt.

It took maybe ten minutes, but at last they were within half a metre of the Pantheon's side railing. Like before, Francis's progress had slowed to a crawl.

"You're very brave, doing this," Natasha said.

"I think you have to say that," said Francis. There was a nervous undertone to his voice, a waver to his words. "It's like kids; make a big deal out of nothing so they feel reassured and good about themselves."

"I don't *have* to say anything. But this is a very big thing for you. I *know* you're being brave, and I'm proud of you. Now: do you want to take the last couple of steps, or stop here? I don't mind; it's up to you."

Francis opened his eyes. They had alternated between jammed shut and open just fractionally. Whenever they were open, he'd pointed them up, staring at the Pantheon's fins and the evening sky, awash with pink. But now he pointed them straight forward, to rest on the railing—and past it, miles and miles of nothing.

"I can do this," he said.

"You can."

He gave a resolute nod. "Last couple of steps, then."

They took one. The second step died and Francis inched backward. For a fleeting second he thought he was in danger of overbalancing, but Natasha had him by the arm and his footing was sure.

He breathed long and deep. "Okay."

Natasha: "Okay?"

"Last step."

It was more of a lurch, really, but he made it nonetheless—*they* made it. He was stood on the very edge of the ship; could reach out and touch the rails. In fact—

"Here," said Natasha. She unwound her arm, then took each of Francis's wrists. Gently, she moved his arms forward, closing the gap, until his hands rested on cold metal. Instantly his fingers curled into an iron grip. Yet still Natasha held on, and as the seconds passed he felt the tension in his hands loosen, just minutely.

"Going to open your eyes?" Natasha asked. "Again, you don't have to."

Another heave of a breath. "Okay."

Prying them open now was the hardest it had ever been. Yet somehow he managed, and after the blur cleared Francis found himself staring out into soft pastels, a faint streak of cloud painted below, and beneath that, land: great and rolling, but averaged out into a flat patchwork quilt of textures and colours. What had once been home.

His breath came out in a whisper. "Wow."

"Majestic, isn't it?" Natasha said. "Sometimes I come up here just to look out; organise my thoughts. It's rather beautiful."

Majestic, beautiful: two words that summed it up perfectly. Better than any Francis could have chosen.

"It all seemed so plain," he said.

"Hm?"

"Down there. It was just … normal. But from up here …" Francis's words trailed off. His eyes scanned. He wondered what direction they were going; how far he'd been carried from home. Would his house be somewhere within view? His parents?

No. They were someone else, far, far behind.

"I'd like to go back to the middle now."

Back they went. Beneath the closest fin, a half-dozen metres behind the porthole, they sat, Francis leaned against one side of the strut and Natasha perched next to him, long legs crossed.

"You did really well, Francis," she said. "I'm really, honestly proud of you."

He pulled a small smile. "Thanks for being there with me. You're better than her, you know?"

"Ruby?"

Francis nodded. "She just forced me—dragged me. You're patient. Thanks for that."

"Think nothing of it. Just looking out for a friend."

They sat in silence for a while, watching. There was still fear in Francis's chest, but it had lessened. Now it was manageable; now he thought he could stand by the railing again, for longer. Not peering *down*—that would be madness—but out, certainly.

A soft breeze whispered through. Overhead, the Pantheon's fins twitched, and the landscape began to slowly shift to one side.

"Course refinement," Natasha said, glancing up. "That'll be Sia, I should think.

"So, you found Mikhail then?"

"I did."

"I saw you all at lunch," Natasha said.

Francis frowned. "Did you?" He racked his brain; he'd been looking out for Natasha, but hadn't spotted her. "Where were you?"

"Just stepped in for a moment. I'm steeped in reports right now, so didn't have much time to stop and eat. Besides, you looked like you were having fun. First time I've seen you laughing, I think."

"They're good guys. I like them."

"Were you plugging the drainage holes?"

Francis filled her in on the morning and afternoon, and his passing adequacy at the task. Natasha laughed when he told her about the glob of sealant that had fallen straight through the hole on his second attempt, and he found himself laughing along with her.

"Are you helping them tomorrow?"

"No; they're going to smooth the plugs on the outer hull, and patch up the wood," Francis said.

"Ah. Not quite ready to hang on a platform beneath the ship, then?"

"Not yet."

Natasha grinned. "I'm sure you'll work up to it."

Francis smirked. "I hope not."

They talked aimlessly for a while longer, the sun sinking lower down; directly ahead, it hung behind the Pantheon's railing, a vibrant orange disc. Francis had to cover his face with his hand, it was so bright, and found himself looking out over the right side of the deck instead.

At first he didn't see it; colours muted, his head either didn't know what he was looking at, or convinced him it was part of the background. But suddenly something clicked; his eyebrows drew down, and whatever had just been coming from his mouth was lost.

"What's that?"

Natasha turned and followed his gaze. "Floating island. A chain, actually."

Francis gaped. From this far off it was difficult to discern, but he thought he could make out rock, and above that, greenery.

"You want to take a closer look?" Natasha asked.

"Err—"

"Sit tight." And without another word, she was up on her legs, over the deck and down the porthole.

A couple of minutes later she was back, something stuffed

under her arm. As she approached, she retrieved it: a long copper telescope, adorned with decorative rings and dotted with dials. Sticking out her free hand, she said, "Come on."

Francis let her pull him up, and they crossed to the opposite rail. This time Natasha didn't take Francis by the arm. Still, she slowed as Francis did, until they were a couple of metres from the Pantheon's edge.

"Staying here?" she asked.

"I think so. And—I mean, that's a telescope."

Natasha grinned. "Right you are. Let me just …"

She placed it to her eye and set about adjusting it, twisting several sections in turn and pausing for a moment to scrutinise one of the dials. When she was happy, she made a pleased noise, and handed it over.

"Go ahead, take a look."

Francis obeyed.

What he saw was breathtaking. The blurry smear he'd spotted a moment ago held nothing compared to the view Natasha presented him with now.

It was indeed a chain: six great rocks strung together by thick runners of what could have been little more than ivy through the viewfinder. Yet Francis suspected it was something thicker by many times, to be visible from this far off: like the trunk of a tree, or perhaps wider.

The rocks were arranged in a cluster, the largest right in the centre. Green topped them all in varying hues. Other patches of colour were just about visible; flowers, probably, like the *charis* in Vala and Stefan's quarters. A handful of dots were moving between the islands, and Francis's mouth dropped when he realised that those tiny specks could only be birds.

But the middlemost island was the most spectacular. Whereas the others were somewhat rounded, this one towered up. A great cleft was worn through the mountain. Mist surrounded it, rendering much of the island invisible—and beneath that cascaded a ribbon of water, spilling over the island's edge and then turning into a spray of mist.

"What—how—"

Natasha laughed. "Which bit?"

"The waterfall."

"Water vapour condenses in the mountain, then pours down a valley and over the edge."

Francis let the telescope rove across the formation, drinking in every little detail; the wear to the rocks, their haphazard shapes, the fragility of it all.

"And there are Volum in there?" he asked.

"Yep. A colony, I'd expect," Natasha said. "Probably other things too. Do you have puceals down there?"

Francis shook his head.

"They're fat little birds with gaping mouths," Natasha explained. "Eyeless, and without legs, so they never roost. Well, that's a puceal. Small, but they taste delicious. We catch them sometimes, when we're running low on food—if we can get close enough. They live around the rocks."

"How do they lay eggs?"

"In each other's mouths." A look of horror passed over Francis's face. "The other option is to drop them and hope for the best. Which would you pick?"

"I'd carry on being human," Francis answered, and Natasha laughed again. He was watching those birds now, the puceals, as they fluttered between places. Natasha was right: no matter how he tracked, they never did seem to stop to land, instead pirouetting in another direction whenever they got too close to the nearest island.

"I should probably let you take a turn," Francis said at last, handing the telescope back across. "It'll be dark soon."

"I've seen it all before," said Natasha, but she placed the viewfinder to her eye and peered out nonetheless. "Interesting little places. Fun to explore, though we rarely find anything of much use. Mostly they're good for restocking the pantry." She paused and swept around, away from the floating islands, looking out over the land. "Vala harvests the plants, too; can make salves with some of them, and others are valuable if you can cultivate them."

Francis thought back to her quarters and its abundance of flora. "Is she a botanist?"

"Botanist, medicine lady, seamstress ... Does it all. We've all got handy hidden talents," Natasha said, and gave Francis a sidelong look. "I expect you have a few of your own, too. Perhaps not filling holes," she added jokingly, "but something."

For a couple moments longer she looked out, then removed the telescope and stuffed it back under her arm. Considering the sky, she rubbed her hands together. "I expect food's about to be served," she said. "Shall we go?"

"Okay."

They returned across the deck, heading for the porthole. Natasha hummed to herself; Francis glanced back at the floating islands. Now he'd seen them through the telescope, he thought he could just about pick out each of the separate pieces ... or maybe that was just his eyes playing tricks on him.

"What exactly do you do on this ship?" Francis asked. "Not *you*, but the ship as a whole."

"Travel; adventure. We don't tend to stay in one place very long. Little bit of trade here and there, but mostly ..." Natasha shrugged. "I suppose our trek to find this fabled 'Ghost Armada' is a prime example, albeit a rather extreme one. We don't hunt ghosts often." She smiled. Now at the porthole, she extended the telescope to Francis; he took it, and she lowered herself onto the ladder. "Mostly we just try to do the same as anyone else in our position."

"Which is?"

"Staying alive."

Her face disappeared below the porthole. A grim twist shook Francis's stomach. Once again, he remembered the last time he'd been out here. How he'd been grabbed from behind. The press of metal against his head.

This was a dangerous world he'd been thrown into. And foreboding though Natasha's words were, he was thankful for the reminder.

Combustion

(Chapter Ten)

1

For a man whose office had once been a grand mahogany room, packed with fine art and sculptures and some of the most exotic plants one could find, an expansive custom-made desk filled with potent cigars, and great wall-to-ceiling windows overlooking the bustling SkyPort he had grown from little more than a handful of stalls, the office Rhod Stein now possessed was almost worse than having nothing at all.

It was small, pokey, stained; what was once a staff room in a store called The Wax Emporium, a shop that sold *candles*, of all things. Candles and potpourri. So it absolutely *stunk*. How anyone found this stuff pleasant was beyond Rhod. To him it was fetid, manufactured. Vile.

He'd considered moving. But in spite of its rancid scent and minimal space, this place had benefits. It was close enough to the clean-up op that Rhod could watch its progress day in, day out (and he'd been doing a *lot* of that). It was also close enough to a thick bundle of cabling running from engineering up to ground level that his men had been able to fashion a work-around, meaning when the *Eden's* power went off, Rhod's stayed on.

Most of the time, anyway.

He could have had them spend longer and set it up elsewhere. Maybe should have. But he'd been in a rush—and besides, the more time they spent fussing about his personal circumstances, the less time they were working on the truly important thing: getting the *Eden* back into shape so she could be reopened and trade could resume.

Rhod's radio clicked. He lifted it from his belt.

"Stein."

"Ah, Mr Stein; it's Lance."

Lance. How Rhod hated this man.

"Good to finally hear from you," Rhod said.

"I have a few minutes to spare and wondered if you'd like to take that meeting now?"

For days now Rhod had been trying to arrange this meeting, but Lance was always too busy. Finally Rhod had passed on his radio frequency so the foreman could get in contact, because damn if he was going to chase Lance around any longer.

"I'll be right out."

The *Eden*'s ground level was less of a mess now. Rubble cleared away, the process of repairing the damage had slowly begun. But it was tedious: given the poor state of the surviving horseshoe of shops, huge sections had to be dismantled before true repair could begin. In order to move forward, they were moving *back* a step.

Ships moved about overhead. On one side of the *Eden*, an enormous crane had been mounted; it was slowly lifting a girder away from the SkyPort, to be jetted off to be recycled. Dozens and dozens of men and women filled ground level. Rhod recognised their faces, but for the wrong reasons: very few of these were the *Eden*'s crew. Most were hired help, burning a fat hole in his bank account.

Beside a fountain that was no longer running stood Lance. His hard hat was tucked under one arm. Dusty overalls hung beneath a face that was too boyish and handsome for Rhod to respect. This was a foreman, not a damned model.

"Lance," Rhod huffed.

Lance turned. A smile broke his face. "Mr Stein." He extended a hand. Rhod looked at it sourly, but shook regardless. "Pleasure to see you again."

"It ought to be. I've been trying to reach you for days."

"Well, things are proceeding rather nicely," Lance said. "We've deconstructed—"

"I'm not after a status report," Rhod cut across. "I want to know how long it will be until I can reopen."

"Ah. Ah, ah, ah." Lance rubbed his chin slowly—infuriatingly. "It'll be a little while longer, I'm afraid."

"How long?"

Lance considered. Spent too long considering. Moments before Rhod thought he might grab the man and shake the answer out of him, Lance said, "Perhaps a fortnight; maybe more."

"A *fortnight*? *Two weeks*?"

"There's still a lot of work to do. This Celeste woman, she did a *lot* of damage. You ought to think about organising a defense strategy in case something like this happens again."

Rhod fumed. Purple crept into his cheeks. "That's *two weeks' worth of trade I've got to lose*. I've already lost customers! Have you seen how many people I've turned away? Why can't I run the functioning part of the port?"

"Intermittent power doesn't really make that possible," Lance said. "And, if you don't mind me saying," he added, "you're somewhat understaffed right now. How many people fled the *Eden* in the fray? I've heard as many as half—"

Rhod roared. It echoed across the plaza. Heads turned and stared before resuming their work, the hum of chatter slowly restarting.

Lance looked taken aback. Nothing more. No fear; just a little surprised. *God*, how Rhod *hated* him.

"Carry on with your work," Rhod growled at last, bending forward and getting right into the man's face. "And hurry the hell up fixing this mess."

He marched away.

2

There had to be something Rhod could take his anger out on.

There was: the candles in this stupid, *stupid* shop. The moment he stepped in he let out another ear-piercing cry and began flinging them from the shelves. Glass holders smashed. Loose candles exploded in showers of wax. Potpourri flew in all directions, crunching underfoot as Rhod wheeled in mad circles, not sure where to direct his hate next.

And then that name clicked in his mind: Celeste. Said through the mouth of a person he despised, it sounded worse somehow.

Baring his teeth like a dog, Rhod pushed into the back room. He hefted down into his chair hard, picked up the phone, and began to dial.

"Hello."

"Imelda," he sneered.

"Ah, Rhod," she said. Like Lance, she sounded too cheerful— too *smug*. "You sound unhappy."

"Don't fuck me around," said Rhod. "It's been *three days* since you called to say your man failed to kill Celeste—*three days*! Have you found her yet or not?"

"Not yet."

"I thought you had her vector!"

"Well she must have changed direction," Imelda snapped back. "Keep your cool, Stein."

"You're meant to know what you're doing! I said I want her head on a damn stick, *so find her and get me it*!"

Rhod slammed the phone down. Panting hard, cheeks flushed, he glared at it—then ripped it up, pulling until the cord went taut, then snapped. The handset was thrown across the tiny room; it smashed into the wall, plastic splitting open, and clattered to the floor in a broken heap.

Rhod breathed hard. Celeste had done this, confined him to this pointless little waste-of-space room. Had ruined him.

But Imelda's men would find her. They had better, the amount he was paying that old witch. And if they didn't …

His fist clenched so hard the knuckles went white. Rhod would get Celeste—no matter what it took.

Diagnostics

(Chapter Eleven)

1

The jobs Francis had been handed over the past couple of days were varied, and sometimes few and far between. Mikhail tried light-heartedly to goad him into assisting with repairs to the Pantheon's outer hull, but Francis couldn't be swayed. He was glad of that: the first evening in the cafeteria, Evans and Peters recounted the fight they'd had on the platform hung over the edge of the ship, and how close Evans had come to taking a misstep over the side. Mikhail had caught him, and they'd all had a good laugh. For Francis, the thought only made him cringe.

One job came to be regular: morning, noon and night, he carted supplies from the pantry up to the kitchen for Samuel. It meant waking up earlier than the majority of the ship, but it also meant he kept busy—and got an early look at the day's eating.

Today, five days after encountering the Modicum, breakfast was scrambled egg, hash browns, beans and toast. It was all written down on a greasy piece of paper, handed to him by Samuel as he walked into the cafeteria.

"No mushrooms?" Francis asked, scrutinising the list. "Bacon?"

Samuel just grunted.

Francis smiled as he headed for the lower deck. An oddity, to be sure, but Samuel had grown on him. He was simple, slow, and didn't talk much. Didn't talk at all, in fact: his vocabulary seemed entirely composed of caveman noises. The fact that he could write had turned out to be quite a surprise, uneven though the scrawl was. He often misspelled words, too, and either had his 'N's backward or drew very disjointed lower-case ones.

Reaching the lower deck, the lights overhead flickered. First just a twitch, then the waver became more violent. Francis paused on the stairs. Finally there was a *pop* and a bulb blew, casting a dim pool beneath it.

He took the last few steps more slowly, wondering if there would be a repeat. But there wasn't; the dead bulb simply sat lifeless, the rest unaffected. Francis peered at the broken light as he passed, and stopped. Maybe it had got too hot?

He poked it. Perhaps not.

With a shrug, he went on.

The pantry was tucked to one side of the Pantheon's lower deck, around a small bend that opened out. Francis turned the corner—

He froze.

A man stood up ahead. In the centre of the floor, his back was to Francis, head bowed slightly forward. The hair on the back of his head was grizzled, and his clothes were full of creases.

"Ben?"

The man turned. His eyes were trance-like. For a second the two stared at each other. Then Benjamin blinked, slow, and as if he had just awoken, the fug ebbed away.

Francis had only seen him on a couple of occasions, and he accepted that Ben always looked as if he forgot to care for himself. But it wasn't just untidy hair or creased clothes now, nor a rug of forgotten stubble. Ben looked downright bedraggled: his clothes weren't just creased but *dirty*, and deep black rings underlined his eyes. Already skinny, his cheeks had taken on a hollow, empty appearance.

"Ben? Are you okay?"

Ben gave a mechanical nod. "Yes. Yes, fine." Even his voice seemed different, as though he'd forgotten how to use his vocal cords. Another of those slow blinks, and the fog in his eyes was diminished further. He took a deep breath. "I'm fine. Just stretching my legs." There: he sounded better now. "Tired, that's all."

They stood still for a moment longer, both considering the other, before Benjamin crossed the floor and headed back for the Volum room.

"Is everything okay in there?" Francis asked.

"Yes."

Ben took the door's handle, then stopped.

Francis waited. But Ben didn't move. Didn't even seem to be breathing.

"Ben?" Francis prompted.

"Yes." Ben looked around. His eyes met Francis's: watery and blue, ringed with darkness.

"I think you're working too hard. Maybe you ought to get some sleep."

It looked like Ben might answer, but when he opened his mouth no words came out. His jaw flapped for a second. Then his eyes steeled.

"Don't come in here."

And with that, the door was open, he was through, and it was closed again, all before Francis could catch even a glimpse into the Volum room's confines.

What a strange man. Francis wondered if he ought to tell someone. Then again, was this par for the course with Benjamin? The entire crew found him strange.

Francis headed into the pantry. It was well-stocked, metal shelves packed with boxes. To one end was a walled-off section with a great steel door: the freezers. Outside was a small rack where meat was hung to defrost. This morning it held the clear plastic bag of puceal breasts Francis had set out last night.

Rechecking the list, Francis began to shift through boxes. Potatoes and onions first, for the hash browns, then beans. The toast was taken care of; Samuel baked that in great batches. Francis had watched one day. For such a heavy-handed man, the loaves came out wonderfully.

It was just a mystery what happened between oven and plate.

The eggs would be last, just in case Francis tripped and smashed the lot. It hadn't happened yet, but that was an unwritten rule with eggs: sooner or later, it would.

As he shifted boxes, he frowned. He paused, pushing a crate of carrots over. There, on the wall behind the racks. It was exposed steel, like the rest of the Pantheon's bottom deck. A bloom of reddish-brown had sprouted.

Francis touched it, then scratched at it. It flaked off.

"Hm. Rust."

"What?"

Francis jerked and spun, knocking carrots in an arc across the pantry floor. Framed in the doorway was Ruby Celeste. For all the shock Francis had felt, she looked downright bored.

"You scared me to death," he said. He held his racing chest.

"So I see. What are you doing down here?"

"Gathering ingredients for Sam."

"What's that got to do with the ship's hull?"

"I ... it's rusting." He moved to one side so she could see. Ruby merely glanced at the patch Francis had uncovered, then fixed back upon him.

"I see."

Was she suspicious? There was that air about her. Of what?

Well, two could play at that.

"What are *you* doing down here?" Francis asked.

An eyebrow rose on Ruby's face. "This is my ship."

"Seems like you're skulking, to me."

"Well, then. It's fortunate that as the Pantheon belongs to me, I am entitled to *skulk*." She drew the word out, enunciating each and every letter. Then, with a cursory glance about the pantry, she turned. "Pick up those carrots, please."

Francis fumed. What was her problem? She'd gone from trying to toss him into every shitty situation the ship had faced, to callous and distrustful. How could everyone on this ship be so nice and normal except for its captain?

Well. He'd get off a jibe of his own. Storming across the room, he poked his head out into the corridor.

"I'd give Benjamin a break, if I were you," he called to Ruby's retreating back. She paused and half-turned. Listening. Good. "I think you're overworking him." He almost tacked on something about the wild goose chase Ruby had them going on, but couldn't. So it was less of a jibe and more looking out for a fellow crewmate. *Good one, Francis,* he cajoled. "Oh, and a bulb blew too. Might want to get that fixed."

Ruby considered the door to the Volum room. "Noted." And without a further word, she walked away.

2

A knock sounded at Ruby's door. "Come in," she said.

Natasha Brady stepped inside. "You wanted to see me."

"I did." Ruby closed the diary—that ever-present diary—and sat forward. "Could you close the door?" When Natasha had, she waved the navigation leader into the seat she usually reserved for Trove, on the rare occasions he was in here.

"How has your morning gone?" Ruby asked. It was small-talk, but also pertinent. Ah, the life of a captain.

"Well. Okay." Natasha heaved a breath. "Could be better."

"Oh?"

"I don't know why, but our progress is dropping off. We should be at least twelve miles further along than we are. It's not much of a difference, but still, our speed is down from yesterday morning, and again the morning before."

"Have you run diagnostics?" Thinking again of Francis's words this morning, Ruby added, "The Volum?"

"I think it's a thrust issue. We're usually running at about ninety percent, but this morning it's hovering around eighty-eight. Eighty-nine yesterday. Perhaps it's a battery problem, seeing as we're still operating on one. But the batteries don't power our thrust, so …" Natasha trailed off. A distracted hand raked through her hair. With a sigh, she unfolded and refolded her legs. "Sia's running diagnostics now to figure out whether cabling has come loose somewhere. I think it may have; the bulb in my quarters keeps flickering."

That brought Ruby's thoughts back to Francis again. She pulled the best smile she could, unpleasant though she felt in her stomach. "When you find the issue, have Mikhail take care of it. Just him and Peters, though; I want Evans to keep up work on the condenser."

"Still not working?"

"No. And the hull has started to rust, too, despite our best efforts."

Indeed it had: whilst breakfast was in progress, Ruby had dismissed Trove, headed down to the bottom deck alone and scoured for flaking metal. Flower-like patches bloomed here and there. The rust had scratched off easily enough, but needed a proper scrub, and then the hull needed to be treated to stop it blossoming again. That was what Mikhail and Peters were on today.

She'd also tried to check in on Benjamin, as per Paige's advice. It had been largely unsuccessful; a few words through the barely-opened door, and then he was gone, back to scrawling and studying and whatever else he did in there. A smell had crept through the crack, a touch unpleasant, but nothing Ruby could recognise through their brief conversation. Probably Benjamin wasn't washing. She'd have to remind him about that next time he extricated himself from the Volum.

"Anyway," Ruby said. "I wondered if I could speak to you about Francis."

A suspicious look crossed Natasha's face. "Yes?"

"What's he doing?"

"What do you mean?"

"For days he spent all his time either shut up in his room, or staring idly at books in the library. Now all of a sudden he's everywhere."

"He wanted jobs to do, so I guess the guys found him some."

"Hm."

"He's a member of the crew now," said Natasha. "Isn't it for the best? You wanted a deckhand—well, Francis is helping out."

"I see."

There was a strained silence. Natasha's answer sounded good on the outside, but ... Ruby still couldn't get the other night out of her head. Francis had led an assassin directly to her door, whether held at gunpoint or not. A ruse? Maybe. And now he was ... what? Was it really as simple as Natasha made out? Ruby wanted to think so, but ...

"I had one other question," she said, trying to brush the tension aside. "I don't really expect anyone will know, but you're the best-read person on the Pantheon, so maybe you've encountered something in your reading.

"How would one go about killing a ghost?"

Natasha's face blanked. She opened her mouth; there was a momentary hesitation before the words came out. Probably working out how best to be tactful, Ruby thought.

"I'm afraid I've never come across anything about that. Supposing ghosts exist, that is—which I rather think they don't."

"But this Ghost Armada ..." The diary was already in Ruby's hands, flipped open to that final page and its manic scrawl. She considered the words hungrily—then snapped it closed and set it aside. "Yes. I expect you're probably right." She flashed Natasha a grin that wasn't entirely earnest. "Well, that'll be all."

Natasha rose. "Good to see you."

"And you. I've been rather evasive lately, haven't I." It wasn't a question, but they both knew she had, and both knew why: their eyes fell upon the diary at the same moment. "Keep me posted regarding our progress, and whether you find the fault."

"Will do."

Natasha departed. Before the door was even closed, the diary was back in Ruby's hands, open to that last page again. She'd read it cover to cover dozens of times now, learned as much from it as she could. If only there were more.

Ghost Armada.

Were these the words of a madman? Surely they were; everyone thought so. And *ghosts*?

But those co-ordinates danced tauntingly beneath.

She just had to know. She had to find out.

3

Francis spent dinner with Mikhail and Peters. Evans was still working on the condenser, to his increased frustration. He turned up just as Francis was leaving, to a hearty guffaw from Peters; Samuel had just packed away the serving station.

"Come on, Sam, you must have something left," Evans begged. "Bit of toast, anything. I'm starving here. Been working all day."

Francis left the cafeteria with a small grin. He wondered how that exchange would turn out.

Natasha hadn't showed, so he followed the corridors until he came to the Pantheon's control room. Its door was open again today. He poked his head in. There she was, frowning at her display. The rest of the room was empty.

"You missed dinner," Francis said.

Natasha looked up. "Oh, did I? Is there anything still out?"

"Sam just packed it up. But Reuben was late, and he's badgering Sam now, so if you're quick …" Francis perched down on one of the free seats and drummed his hands. The display in front of him scrolled information. He didn't even try to make sense of it.

"Eh, I'll leave it." Natasha sighed. "Fancy distracting me?"

"I thought that's what I was doing."

"Hah. Come on, let's get out of here. I've had enough of diagnostic reports for one day."

"Library?" Francis suggested.

"Go for it."

They strolled through the ship and headed up the stairs, making small-talk. Though she was tense, Natasha took it well, yet something was clearly on her mind. When they were sat, Francis would ask if she wanted to talk about it.

But today the library wasn't unoccupied. Stood in the middle of the floor, eyes flying furiously back and forth across the page of a thin book, was—

"Benjamin?"

He looked up. Alarm creased his face.

"Miss Brady. I was just—" He moved to stuff the book into its place on the shelf. It missed, flapping sideways, and fell from his hand. Ben didn't bother trying to pick it up; instead he sped across the room. Two feet from the doorway, he jerked to a stop. His eyes seemed to cloud.

"I haven't seen you in *days*," said Natasha.

Ben didn't answer. Didn't even look. He merely stared straight ahead, somewhere between Francis and Natasha. Francis glanced at the navigation leader, looked backward. The hall was empty. His lips pursed.

"Is everything okay?" Natasha asked.

That seemed to rouse Ben. He blinked. "Yes." Then he stepped past the two and hurried up the corridor. An unpleasant smell wafted behind him.

"Hey, wait!" Natasha shouted. "Ben, is everything okay with the Volum?"

Again, he froze. "It's fine," he said. "Don't come down there!"

And then he was gone, Francis and Natasha staring perplexedly after him.

"What was that about?" Natasha asked.

"I don't know." Francis stepped into the room. A strange odour hung in the air. It was faint and metallic, with a hint of rot. He wrinkled his nose, then stooped to pick up Ben's discarded book. "I saw him this morning, too. Is he usually like that?"

"No," Natasha answered. She sank into one of the plush seats and idly spun the globe beside it. "What was he reading?"

Francis showed her the cover. "Book about engineering."

"Random."

"Hm." He pushed it back into its hole on the shelf. "So what was that about the Volum?"

"Ah, navigation issue," said Natasha. "Nothing too important; we're just moving a little slower than we ought."

Francis nodded. He sat. "Those reports?"

"That'll be it." Natasha grinned. "Anyhow, I want distracting, not thinking about faulty cables."

He shouldn't push it, but: "Faulty cables? Would that make the lights flicker?"

"Yours too?"

Francis nodded.

"Probably. But the reports are … weird." Natasha pulled a face. "Apparently *all* of the cables on the ship are operating at a reduced capacity, but our consoles didn't give us any indication."

Francis considered. "When the Modicum hit, maybe?"

"Could've knocked some loose, but not like this."

"Hm."

Natasha thought for a few moments longer. Then she shook her head, spun the globe again. "I'm finished for the day now. No sense thinking about it any longer. It's a problem for tomorrow. So: find me a book, and make it a good one. If you're lucky I'll read you the best bits."

4

It was another two days later, when Francis was midway through his morning, that an alarm sounded across the Pantheon. He looked up from his diary and frowned. This klaxon was different to the one that had sounded after the Modicum attacked, but familiar. Then he remembered: it was used to announce a meeting in the canteen.

Half the crew had amassed when Francis arrived. Today the growing formation was headed by Ruby, Trove, and Mikhail. Mikhail looked somewhat troubled.

"Morning," Francis whispered to Natasha as he slotted in beside her. "Any clue what's going on?"

"None," she answered.

It took less than a minute for the final few crew members to arrive.

"Minus Benjamin?" Ruby muttered. She pulled an irritated face and shook her head. "Never mind; we'll talk to him later. Go ahead, Mikhail."

"Morning, everyone," said Mikhail. "I appreciate you gathering here at short notice. This is a little unexpected, but important. This morning, during a routine inventory check, I found us short on sealant. For those of you that might not know, it's the stuff we use to bond holes in the hull. Last time it was used there were around twenty kilos of the stuff left—this morning we're down to sixteen. What that means …"

"What that *means*," Ruby took over, stepping forward, "is one of two things. Either Mikhail made a counting error after he and his team finished patching up the ship's holes. Or there is a thief aboard the Pantheon." She paused and let her eyes drift over the crew. They seemed to linger half an instant longer than necessary on Francis, before sweeping off elsewhere. "Regardless, our concern is simply return of the … shall we say 'misplaced' materials. If any of you happens to know their whereabouts, maybe took them, replace them at your earliest availability.

"If the items are returned, no questions will be asked. However." Ruby held up a finger. "If in twenty-four hours it has *not* been replaced, a full search of the ship will be conducted. Then I *will* be asking questions."

There was another pause as that sunk in. No murmurs. After Ruby was content, she nodded. "Dismissed."

Chatter started, and everyone began to file out of the canteen. Francis wandered alongside Natasha, who looked troubled herself, now he thought about it. He had just opened his mouth to ask what was wrong when a voice from behind called, "Hey, Francis."

He turned. Mikhail headed up the corridor. He wore an uneasy smile.

"Hey," said Francis. "Weird, huh?"

"Yeah, little bit." Mikhail rubbed the back of his neck. "Listen, you haven't seen anything, have you? You're down there a fair bit."

"Not a thing," Francis said. He paused and added, "Well, I've seen Benjamin out and about a couple of times, but never doing anything. Bit vacant. I think maybe he's overworked. I mentioned to Ruby, but …"

"Nothing else? Nothing suspicious?"

"Not a thing."

Relief split Mikhail's features. "Good. Phew. I didn't think so—and I definitely don't think you took it, if you wondered. The captain, she's just … a little jumpy right now." He waved the thought aside. "Thanks for letting me know."

"No problem."

Mikhail checked the clock on his communicator. "I'd better get on," he said. "Inventorying today—don't suppose you're up for it?"

"Ah, no, thanks. I have some writing to finish."

"Oh. Novelist?"

Francis laughed. "Just a diary."

"Okay. I won't keep you. Probably for the best, anyway, given Miss Celeste's jumpiness. Enjoy your day."

Off he went, back up the corridor. Francis turned to follow on with Natasha—but she was gone too. His lips pulled into a tight line. Perhaps he'd find out what was up with her later instead.

5

But though Francis thought he might get a moment to talk with Natasha at lunch, he didn't: she didn't appear in the canteen. Neither did Mikhail or the others, so Francis parked by Vala and Stefan and listened to them bicker in their usual light-hearted manner.

Natasha wasn't at dinner, either: not on her usual table, not anywhere in the bustling room. Frowning, Francis wandered to the queueless serving station. "Evening, Sam," he said, to a grunted reply.

After Sam had filled his plate with mashed potatoes, peas, half a puceal breast and a thin covering of watery gravy, Francis wove through the tables and sat on the free one beside Mikhail, Evans, Peters and Herschel.

"Evening," Mikhail said, breaking from whatever the others were laughing about, and leaning over the back of his chair. "How'd your writing go?"

"Fine," said Francis. "How about inventorying?"

"Almost finished. Easy job when there's four of you. Would've been easier if we had five."

"Yeah," Evans added. "You could've recounted everything Glim here was on. Or offered an extra set of hands for when he ran out of fingers and toes."

They laughed, then carried on their conversation.

"I had another question for you, actually," Mikhail said. Speaking lower now, he continued, "You mentioned seeing Ben a couple of times?"

"Yeah?"

"How did he seem? You said he was a bit vacant?"

Francis chewed a piece of puceal smeared with mashed potato and swallowed. "Yeah, kind of. Seemed a bit … I don't know, jerky. As if his brain wasn't quite switched on." He pushed peas onto his fork with his knife. "Why?"

"He came out earlier. I thought he was going to shout at us because these two were making such a racket. But …" Mikhail's brow creased. "He just stood there and stared at the wall. Seemed funny at first, but I spoke to him and he was just …" He waved his hands. "Like you said. Like his brain wasn't quite switched on."

"Maybe he's overworked. I mentioned it to Ruby, but I guess she hasn't done anything." Not that that surprised Francis. She was obviously so single-mindedly focused on finding this Ghost Armada she had Ben breaking his back to get them there as fast as possible, never mind the consequences to the man's sanity.

"Maybe," said Mikhail.

"Did you say something about Ben?"

They looked around. Vala leaned forward, listening curiously.

Mikhail: "Yeah, why?"

"I saw him yesterday. Well, we did, didn't we?"

Stefan gave his wife an obligatory nod and carried on eating.

"I thought it was a bit weird, seeing how rare it is to see him outside. Thought it was even weirder when I realised he was staring into space. Just frozen, like a statue. Creepy, wasn't it?" She looked to Stefan for support; another nod.

"Is he okay?" Vala asked. "Stefan here tried to speak to him, but he was just kind of blank and slow. Then he hurried off muttering something about not going down there."

"He means the Volum room," Mikhail said. "He told me that, too."

"And me," Francis added.

"He's protective of that thing," said Mikhail. "Still, kind of weird, isn't it?"

Vala glanced around. Leaning further forward, she pressed a hand to one side of her mouth and whispered, "He smelled funny. I don't think he's been washing."

Francis listened for a while longer as Mikhail and Vala talked. *How odd,* he thought. Clearly Benjamin was already something of a strange man—Francis had had enough indication of that from the rest of the crew. But now his oddness had ramped up enough that his crewmates were taking notice.

Francis glanced around. There was Trove, sat at a table by himself, dinner half-forgotten as he scrutinised his ever-present clipboard. But no Ruby. And that was a shame. If she were around to hear, maybe she would stop pushing Ben so hard.

Or then again, as Francis had already mentioned it to her once before, maybe she wouldn't.

6

A lone voice wafted down the corridor a half-dozen metres before Francis arrived at the control centre.

"Ben? Benjamin? *Benjamin Thoroughgood!*"

Francis loomed at the doorway, plate in hand. He thought maybe he ought not to interrupt, but then changed his mind. He'd brought Natasha dinner, after all, and judging by the irritation in her voice, maybe she could do with it.

Natasha wasn't at her usual station: today she stood in front of the main console, her back to Francis. Her wrist pressed to the side of her face, she jabbed down a button on her communicator and half-yelled, "Benjamin, damn well respond when you're hailed!" There was no reply. "Benjamin Thoroughgood!"

"Maybe you're not shouting loud enough."

Natasha whirled. She let her arm drop and heaved a sigh, then crossed the room and hefted down into her seat. For a few seconds she didn't say anything, merely stared sullenly at her screen. Then she looked at the plate in Francis's hands and said, "That's for me, right?"

He handed it over. "Here you go." From his pocket came cutlery, wrapped in a napkin. "You weren't at lunch or dinner, so I thought I should bring you something."

"Thanks." Plate balanced on her legs, Natasha began to eat. Every now and again she'd glare at her communicator. The rest of the time her eyes were fixed darkly on her screen.

Halfway through the meal, she huffed a breath and placed the plate on top of her workstation. Cutlery banged down, hard. Then she started to scroll through whatever had her attention at the console.

"So," Francis finally said, "what's the problem?"

"Nothing."

"I don't believe that."

"Well, it doesn't matter. Can't get the right people to pay attention to the damn thing, so just got to live with it."

"Who's the right people?"

"Ben." For emphasis, Natasha lifted her wrist again, pressed a button and yelled, "Ben! Answer your damn communicator!" Still nothing. She punched the workstation, a heavy metallic clang.

"What about Ruby?"

"Never around."

"Where is she?"

Eyes rolled. "Probably poring over that stupid diary again. Where else?" Natasha stared at the screen. Then she let out another breath, this one more a sigh than a huff, and turned toward Francis. "Thanks for coming out to see me, but I'm pretty stressed right now. It's every man for himself, apparently." She raked fingers through her hair. "I don't feel like talking right now. Sorry. But I've got a day off tomorrow—at long last—so how about we catch up in the morning, right after breakfast? Can sit on the deck; gives me an excuse to get outside instead of spending every waking hour shut in here."

Francis nodded. "Okay, that sounds good." He rose. "I hope you feel better soon."

"Hah. You and me both."

He pointed at the plate. "Want me to take that?"

"Nah," Natasha said. "Might finish it later. When it's stone cold and I'm still no further along. See you tomorrow, Francis."

He left her to herself. Partway up the corridor, her calls for Ben resumed. Judging by the irritation in her voice, and just how far it carried, Francis guessed Ben still wasn't answering.

Overworked. Everyone in this ship was being overworked. Or at least the ones responsible for navigation. And where was the captain?

Nowhere to be found. Unless she had a finger to point.

Francis grimaced. What a surprise.

7

After a somewhat lacking breakfast of beans on toast, Francis and Natasha headed out for the Pantheon's top deck.

"Did you finish the meal last night?" Francis asked.

"Eventually," said Natasha. "Freezing by the time I did, but I ate it nonetheless. Thanks for bringing it over."

"No problem."

"And sorry for being ratty."

"It's okay. You were stressed. Happens. I'm hardly one to talk, am I?"

Natasha gave a little grin at that. "I suppose not."

They climbed the ladder and stepped out. The morning sun was beating down. It would be hot later today, Francis could already tell. Cloud hovered a little way below. It seemed closer this morning, Francis thought as he stopped by the railing to peer.

No floating islands to spy, today. Just cotton wisps and land down below—or, rather, the absence of it, as everywhere Francis looked he saw only blue ocean waters. Not even the head of a tiny island pocked its surface.

"Pretty," he mused.

"Bit boring," said Natasha. "Lot more sea than land down there. We're over this most of the time." She held the railing and leaned forward to stare straight down. "Or some variant thereof. Come on, let's sit."

They plodded back across the deck and took up position under one of the Pantheon's fins, this one near the front of the ship. Francis glanced up at it. Like a great wall terminating in a notched point, it rose high into blue skies.

"So what was up yesterday?" Francis asked.

"It's complicated."

"Try me."

Natasha inhaled. "Okay. We're not making as much progress as we ought to be. And the ship seems to be dropping in altitude. Nothing much," she added at the bolt of alarm that must have crossed Francis's face, "but we're not packing quite the lift we should be. We're generating less power, and I don't know if it's because of the Volum, or if there's something wrong with the ship's circuitry. Loose wires, something like that."

"You said the wires are faulty throughout the whole ship," Francis said.

"I did." Natasha chewed her lip. "But that's impossible. So it must be a computer error. But every time I run diagnostics to try to figure out if there's something wrong with our systems, they're running perfectly. Or they *were*; last night they started bugging out on me too. Error messages."

Francis frowned. Something was going wrong with the Pantheon. They were dropping height—and right over ocean, too. His heart thrummed in his chest. Not outright panic, not yet, but concern. It was a long way down.

"Has anything like this happened before?"

"Now and again. The Pantheon is pretty old. Older than me, definitely older than Ruby. Things don't always run perfectly in a vessel this age—hence why a battery and condenser blew out last week. It's no big deal really, but I haven't been able to speak to Ruby or Ben, and it's stressing me out. I'm in charge of navigation, but the ship isn't giving me what I want out of it."

"Hm." Francis looked out. A rolling puff of cloud loomed ahead; they would pass over it soon. So it *had* looked larger. "We had sunk down into a cloud formation the first morning I was here," he said. "So I guess it's pretty normal, right? No danger?"

"No danger," said Natasha. "Still, I really think we should check in with the nearest SkyPort when we can, get someone more qualified to fix us up. Reuben is great, but the condenser alone has caused him trouble all week; I don't think he'll be much better fixing a full operating system."

"He's still working on that?"

"I think Ruby pulled him off; now it's more of a backburner project. He hasn't had much luck with it. I don't think that's going to change."

"The hull is rusting down there," Francis said. "It's getting pretty bad in places. I never realised how fast that stuff spreads."

"Hm."

They were quiet for a while. Francis watched as the cloud up ahead disappeared below the Pantheon's front rail. A soft creak split the gentle breeze, and he glanced up as the fin above them turned a few degrees left. Course correction.

"So where's the nearest SkyPort?"

"Couple of days out still. *Cacophonous Harmonics*. Little place, by the sound of it, but there'll be someone who can help us out. Just a matter of convincing the captain to make a stop."

A couple of days out. Francis's heart sped.

"We could ask around," he said.

Natasha nodded. "We could."

Footsteps interrupted the thought.

"Ben!" Natasha stood and rounded the fin. Francis scrabbled to his feet and followed. "Ben, I spent *hours* yesterday hailing you! Why didn't you answer?"

Francis stopped in his tracks. Natasha stopped too.

Awful: that was the only way to describe Ben. He stood by the porthole, a half-dozen metres away, glassy-eyed. Stubble was turning into a short matted beard, smeared with something brown. The same streaks covered Ben's clothes, which were more bedraggled than ever: a crisscrossing maze of endless creases and something Francis didn't care to think about. His eyes were pale, the pupils miniscule. Dark rings hung under them. His skin looked papery, both the wrong texture and colour. His jaw was lax, and a runner of saliva had trickled down one corner of the man's downturned lips.

Natasha breathed, "Ben?"

For a second, no response. Then his body jerked—more of a twitch, really, it was so slight—and he blinked. His mouth worked.

"Don't," he said.

He moved, across the deck, heading for the side. There was an instant of doubt in Francis's mind—Natasha's too—and then it clicked for both of them at once. Exactly what Ben was about to do—and they were too many steps away to stop it.

Both flew forward.

Ben hit the railing, lurched sideways, and tumbled end over end and out of sight.

"Ben!" Natasha screamed. She slammed into the rail, held firm. "*Ben!*"

Francis grabbed the railing, bent forward, stared. A body spun, receding—then it was swallowed by white cloud and was gone.

"*Ben!!*"

8

"What *happened*?"

All around was a flurry of voices. The morning's activities had ceased; the entire crew—entire *remaining* crew—had gathered on the top deck, most pressed as close to the railing as possible and looking down through the heavens. There was nothing to see but blue.

"He just came out," said Natasha. Tears streaked her face. She stood alongside Mikhail, whose arm was thrown about her racked shoulders, as well as a pale and shaken Francis, a similarly complexioned Trove, and Ruby. Who, for the first time in days, looked concerned. "I tried to call to him, but he didn't reply, did he?" Francis shook his head. "And then he just … just …" Her words were lost to a hiccough. Mikhail squeezed tighter.

"Did he just fall?" Ruby asked. "Did he *jump*?"

"He wasn't walking properly," Natasha said. "I don't think he could have jumped if he tried. He just kind of lurched."

"But did he do it on purpose, I want to know," said Ruby. She looked at Natasha, but no answer came. Next she stared at Francis. Confused lines wrinkled her forehead. "Did he do it on purpose?"

Francis thought. He'd always read that terrible events seemed to happen in slow-motion. Yet there was no slow-motion replay of

Ben going over the edge. One moment he was there; the next a chaotic tumble of limbs, and then he was simply gone.

"I don't know," he said at last. "Like Natasha said, he just walked at the side and ..." He waved his arms lamely. "Went over."

"There's been something wrong with him for days," Natasha said. "We saw him in the library the other night, and he looked *weird*. And Francis saw him a few mornings ago, didn't you?"

"Yes," he said. "I did." His eyes met Ruby's, and he did everything he could to communicate his vehemence: *I told you he was overworked, you should have listened, and now he's thrown himself into the sea.* She seemed to understand, because her gaze flitted away.

"A few of us saw him," said Mikhail. "He came out yesterday while we were taking inventory. And Vala said she and Stefan saw him."

Ruby was silent.

Trove stepped in. "Perhaps there's a clue in the Volum room. Or his personal quarters."

They exchanged glances. "Worth a look," Mikhail said.

9

The walk through the ship was one of the longest of Francis's life. Every step seemed to last an age. And yet, as the five reached the stairs onto the bottom deck, their journey's conclusion came nonetheless.

Rust had bloomed everywhere. Somehow it seemed *worse* than this morning. Every flower of red had grown, worsened. Flakes of metal littered the floor. Two bulbs were dead. Both had been fine when Francis was gathering ingredients for breakfast.

"This—" he started, but stopped.

They all stopped.

Up ahead, the door to the Volum room. It was shut, as always. And around the edges of the door, inches thick the entire way, was uneven grey: solid and steely, but not steel. Not exactly.

"Well," Mikhail breathed at last. "I think we found what happened to our missing sealant."

A Snippet of Stein

(Chapter Twelve)

The phone rang. Angry thoughts were sidelined.

Rhod broke his stare from the desk. Fat fingers picked up the receiver, pressed it to his ear. "Stein."

A whispery voice answered. "Ah, Rhod." A lilting, gleeful voice he despised.

And yet, she was calling him.

"Imelda. I assume you have news."

"No small talk?" She tutted. "So impolite, Rhod. It's good manners to ask a lady how her day has been."

Rhod's grip tightened on the plastic. "I *assume* you have news," he repeated.

Imelda tittered. "You oughtn't assume. You know the saying." She waited, but Rhod didn't give a snide reply. "Yes, Rhod, you assume correct. I have news."

He leaned forward. Knuckles turned white. "Which is?"

"We've found her."

"*Yes.*"

"I thought you'd be pleased."

"Where?"

"Heading north-west. Within spitting distance of a port called *Cacophonous Harmonics*. I expect that's where she's headed." Imelda paused. "She won't make it."

"See that she doesn't."

"I will."

"Remember—"

"Yes, yes," Imelda cut across, sounding bored. "Head on a stick. I shan't forget. She killed one of my men, after all. The head on the stick is the best part."

The Volum Room

(Chapter Thirteen)

1

Seventeen men and women arranged themselves on the Pantheon's top deck that afternoon: the sixteen remaining crew members, plus Francis. Even the handful of night shift workers were here; a trio of two women and a man whose names Francis didn't know. A couple of people were dressed in black, Ruby included, but only a few. Evidently funeral clothes were in short supply on the Pantheon.

Ruby stood alone at the fore of the group, which was arranged in two uneven lines; Trove had taken up place in the rear row.

"And thus, we bid farewell to Benjamin Thoroughgood: caretaker to our Volum. Often obsessive, irate at interruptions, but a wonderful man who did us proud." Ruby removed her hat. "To Ben."

A sombre chorus followed: "To Ben."

A roar of thunder pocked the afternoon as the six side cannons unloaded a volley. Five seconds passed, then another volley, and a third five seconds later.

Reflective silence for a minute, then Ruby looked up at her crew and replaced the tricorne on her head. They were dismissed with a nod. Slowly, the crowd split into groups and dispersed. Some stayed on the deck—Vala and Stefan wandered arm-in-arm to the front of the ship, where they held each other and looked out— while others headed back inside, filtering down the porthole.

Francis hovered. Natasha, one of the few in full black, was

stood mutely by Mikhail. They'd been relegated to the back row for their height. Francis moved to them now. He pulled a wan smile, which Natasha returned. Mikhail squeezed her shoulder.

"Hi," Francis greeted.

"Hey."

"So what's the plan now?"

"Afternoon off," Mikhail said.

"What about the Volum room?" said Natasha. "There could be something inside we need to see. Some clue as to why …" Her voice quivered.

Mikhail: "I—"

"It'll be easier to get it out of the way. For everyone."

Mikhail considered. He and Francis locked eyes. Francis lifted his shoulders in a minute shrug.

"Okay. We'll do it now. But you don't have to be there for this, Tasha."

"I want to be. I have to know what drove him to this."

"Okay." Mikhail looked to Francis. "You in?"

"Got nothing better to do."

A grin ghosted Mikhail's lips. "That's the spirit. I'll show you how to break through sealant."

"Okay."

Natasha: "We should get Ruby, too. And Trove. They'll want to see as well."

Yes, Francis thought. *I daresay they will.* He risked a look at Ruby. She and Trove stood by the ship's railing. As Francis watched, Ruby sighed, then leaned against the rail and held her head in her hands. Guilt?

He hoped so.

2

Maintenance equipment was housed in the same room as munitions on the Pantheon's bottom deck. Francis had never really been in here, so to step in alongside Mikhail and Natasha—Ruby and Trove would join them later, when they'd succeeded in blasting through the door—was an enlightening experience.

For one, a full side of the room brimmed with cannonballs. Piled onto floor-to-ceiling racks several deep, there had to be enough to last a decade.

Beside was a locked cabinet. Yellowed and faded, a label was stuck to its front: *AMMUNITION*.

Along the other side of the room was the maintenance equipment, arranged on shelving and cabinets. Bottles and cans and tubs and boxes, plus tools of all different shapes and sizes. It was remarkably well ordered, given the mess Francis was accustomed to in the pantry, though maybe that was because Mikhail and his team did a better job of keeping everything in check, compared to shoving things around and throwing carrots across the floor.

But most noticeable:

"It's rusting in here, too," Francis said.

Mikhail didn't look up from his search. "That it is. Nasty stuff. Going to have to spend tomorrow trying to scrub it all off."

Red was everywhere. Some blooms had spread so far their outer edges were touching, connected. One particularly nasty spot looked like a very shallow but wide crater, and when Francis extended a finger, a thin strip of reddened steel coiled up to meet him, then split off and fluttered to the ground.

It had started to swallow the cannonballs, too. Only little flecks so far. And the rack was dotted with brown. And the ammo cabinet—and its lock.

"Why's it so bad?" Francis asked. "I only saw it a few days ago."

"Must be a lot of moisture down here," said Mikhail. "Only got one working condenser, remember; probably isn't doing a good enough job by itself."

"Hm."

This was beginning to get ridiculous. For all Natasha's reassurance that the ship was fine, things seemed to be going wrong an awful lot right now.

"It's like it's eating the ship," Francis said. He had circled the room and was back to that crater. Its mottled centre was like something from a nightmare. He moved to touch it again, but changed his mind.

"That's what rust does. Don't worry; it's aesthetic."

"That doesn't look aesthetic."

Mikhail glanced up at the patch Francis pointed at. "Well, mostly aesthetic then. Spots like that we'll just fill with sealant. Job done. Now—aha. Here we go."

Mikhail rose holding a fat plastic tub, and on top of that, a very small metal container with an oversized lid. The stack was topped by three pairs of thick gloves, a cluster of face masks, and another three pairs of goggles.

"You'll want those. This stuff is nasty."

"What is it?" Francis asked.

"Sort of like the sealant, but has the opposite effect."

"It's also explosive," Natasha added.

"Always ruining the fun," said Mikhail. He stuck his tongue out at Natasha and got a middle finger back, then grinned at Francis. "No need to be wide-eyed. It only explodes a little bit. It's very contained, but pretty powerful. That's what the goggles and gloves are for."

"What about the rest of me?" Francis asked.

"You're responsible for that."

Francis swallowed hard. He'd pictured them chiselling the sealant off somehow, or maybe applying something that could dissolve it. Hell, the way the rust was spreading, maybe they could wait and hope that did the job. Explosives, though?

"And the face masks?"

"It smells."

"Like rot," Natasha clarified.

"Brilliant," Mikhail said. "Now I won't be able to convince him to have a sniff."

"That's the point. Come on, let's get on with it."

They filed out of the room and into the corridor. Now a third bulb had joined the other two dead ones. Mikhail and Natasha carried on as if it were nothing, but Francis grimaced as he passed under this new patch of darkness. Fingers crossed Natasha could convince Ruby to stop by *Cacophonous Harmonics* and get someone to take a look at this mess of a ship.

They donned their protective gear—not that Francis felt particularly protected. Just in case, he hovered near the back of the trio: the extra distance would help in case anything winged his direction. Maybe.

Mikhail squatted and opened the large tub. "This is your base," he said to Francis. It was two-thirds full with something vibrant orange. A wooden stick was dipped in the stuff. At first Francis thought it was like paint, but when Mikhail took the stick and stirred, it was too viscous—*far* too viscous. Even more rubbery than the goo the sealant had started out as.

"I'll get one of these for each of you in a second," Mikhail said.

"Hang on, I'll do it," said Natasha. "Keep explaining to Francis."

"So, this is your base," Mikhail repeated. Now, using this—" he waved the stick "—we apply a tiny amount to the sealant. Only a tiny amount, and *only* the sealant." To emphasise, he fought with the orange rubber for a few seconds, then pulled the stirrer out. It came with a horrid sucking noise. It was dry: not a trace of orange marred it. Then Mikhail dipped the edge of the stick back in, which Francis saw now had a flat, hardened edge, and by pressing toward the edge of the tub was able to separate a coin-sized globule. He lifted it to show Francis the size, then smeared it very carefully into a line against the sealant around the Volum room door.

Natasha came back in and passed Francis his spreader. He nodded his thanks.

"*Now*." Mikhail picked up the metal container. "This stuff." He passed it up to Francis, who took it very, very carefully. "The lid is a combination lock. Only a couple of us know the combo, yours truly included. I'm afraid I won't be sharing it with you."

"Good," Francis said over a nervous laugh. He passed the container back.

"I like the way you think." Mikhail fiddled with the dials, and a few seconds later the lid popped off. "Same deal as the sealant; more powder." A tiny metal scoop was inside this container, and Mikhail lifted it out sporting no more than a few glittering black grains. "Press it against the base, and then wait."

In one fluid motion, he pressed the scoop to the smear of orange. Then he inched back and sat crouched, watching and waiting.

Nothing happened at first. But after ten seconds or so, something sparked—and a moment later there was a tiny, high-pitched explosion and a blinding flash. Francis shut his eyes, threw up his arms.

"Done."

Francis looked. So it was: a patch a few inches wide and a couple deep had been blown in the sealant. The edge of the door wasn't visible yet—there was too much sealant for that still—but with another repeat or two, it would be.

"Highly contained, very small, and vaporises steel. Another reason we've got these face masks." Mikhail looked between Natasha and Francis in turn. "So," he said. "Shall we get started?"

3

Even with the three of them, the task was long and arduous. Francis peeled off briefly to help Samuel collect ingredients for dinner, and then an hour later they all got pause to go up and eat.

The mood in the canteen was sombre. And although Francis had never seen Ben in the cafeteria, today it felt as though there was some gulf left by his absence, as if things in the room weren't quite correct.

Ruby was in attendance today, sitting with Trove. She looked weary. Didn't seem hungry, too; half a plate of pasta sat unfinished before her, quills pushed around but not eaten.

Francis was surprised by his appetite. But breaking through a sealed door with explosives was clearly the kind of job that worked one up, because he wolfed his pasta down and was tempted to ask Samuel for seconds. No need, luckily: Natasha wasn't eating much either, and scooped the rest of hers onto Francis's plate.

"Come on then," she said as soon as Francis had finished his last bite. "Let's get back to it."

It was another three hours before Mikhail finally stepped back from the door and said, "Shall we call Ruby?"

The door was a mess. The edges were battered, wood destroyed by the many blasts, revealing solid steel beneath. Every inch was blackened. Save for a thin seal where the door handle used to be— now only a gaping hole remained—the Volum room was accessible once more. Along with whatever lay inside.

"Okay," said Natasha.

Mikhail thumbed his communicator, touched a couple of buttons. A moment later: "Mikhail?"

"Miss Celeste," he said. "We're almost through."

"I'll be down in a moment."

The three exchanged looks. They had all reeled at what might be inside. What had driven Ben to madness and lured him over the edge of the ship to a watery grave? Francis couldn't even imagine. And now the answer was almost upon him—if indeed there was one. They might open this sealed vault and find nothing more than what Francis had seen on his first day here: the Volum, pulsing light, bags of pellets, and shelves packed full of ledgers.

But then, if that was the case, why seal the room at all?

Mikhail applied the last of the orange goo while they waited, then detonated it.

"We're through."

Tension hung in the air. None of them said a word.

Two pairs of footsteps came from behind.

"Are we ready to go in?" Ruby asked.

Mikhail nodded. "Would you like to?" he offered. But Ruby shook her head, so he said, "Okay then."

He rested a hand on the door. Francis's heart raced.

Pushed.

It swung open.

The smell hit Francis first. Even through his face mask he was assaulted with the stench of effluent. He fought the urge to gag and failed; turning and hurrying away, he yanked the mask aside and vomited. Someone else did the same.

Once he'd finished retching, Francis wiped his mouth on his sleeve and replaced the face mask. The others had gone inside. The only thing was to follow.

The Volum room was a mess. *Defiled*. Excrement smeared the walls, shelves had been trashed, ledgers were everywhere. Across one wall was smeared the word '*INFECTION*'. The same disgusting mural was painted beneath in smaller letters, all written in uneven capitals.

There was rust, too. Somehow it was worse here: it covered every inch of every wall, had snaked across the ceiling, began eating at the cables. Great patches were dimpled, the steel lifting away. Flecks of eaten metal covered the floor. So bad was it that the walls didn't seem to be steel anymore: now they looked unstable, as if the slightest touch would cause the place to fall.

But the *light*, Francis realised. Part of his brain had clocked it the moment the door was open, the same moment his body had to override him and empty its contents on the floor.

The entire room was lit in dull amber. And in the middle, the Volum: still huge, but somehow smaller than Francis remembered, its face downturned, its breathing laboured. No pulsing light came from it: just a steady, low glow.

"It's orange," Francis muttered. "Isn't it meant to be blue?"

A long silence. Then, at last Trove answered, "Yes. That's right."

"So why—"

But Francis didn't get time to finish, because an explosion

rocked the ship. Careening sideways, he crashed into a desk. Wood connected with his head; he grunted as stars exploded across his vision.

"What the hell was that?" Natasha cried.

A familiar alarm began to wail.

From his place on the floor, Francis stared at four ashen faces.

They were being attacked.

The Pantheon, Boarded

(Chapter Fourteen)

1

Voices filled the Pantheon's control centre as Ruby hurtled through the open doorway, Natasha, Trove and Francis behind her. Natasha landed ungracefully at her console and began furiously typing. Trove stood by the door, and Francis hovered next to him, gripping the frame. The ship had been rocked three times more in their sprint up here.

"What's going on?" Ruby demanded. "Camera feeds?"

"Lost all of them," Sia answered. "One through three lost in the blast, four and five appear to be malfunctioning—"

"*What?*"

"—and six is non-responsive."

"What do you mean four and five are malfunctioning? We replaced them just a few days ago."

Sia's hands flew over her keyboard. A moment later the offending feeds popped up on the main display. Their images were garbled. An uneven vertical line drove across camera five's display, filling one half in black.

"What happened?"

"We started encountering issues this morning. This afternoon they were worse, and now—"

Another explosion rocked the ship. The images on screen juddered. Then camera five turned black, and a moment later disappeared entirely.

Sia stared. "I didn't do that."

"Damn it." Ruby spun. "Natasha: change course. Starboard."

"I'm trying, but I've got no nav control," Natasha said. She hammered at the keys, hard lines creasing her forehead. "Did we lose a fin?"

"No," came Amelie's answer. "Schematics show all fins are—"

No explosion, but something huge and heavy crashed up above, loud enough to be heard through steel. Another alarm shrieked, and from the door Francis saw text scroll even faster across Amelie's screen. Something was flashing red.

"Down a fin," Amelie gasped. "The central one; it's *gone*."

Ruby's teeth gritted. "Stefan, I want you to fire all cannons on my mark."

"Miss Celeste, we don't have a vector—"

"*On my mark!*" she cried. "Mark!"

Thunder rumbled the ship as six side cannons and the enormous central cannon fired into the darkness. Ruby repeated the order, and the ship rumbled again as its bowels unloaded.

"Mark," she said.

No sound. She waited an instant. "Mark!"

"I'm trying," said Stefan. "The system isn't letting me—"

Something rumbled, but quieter, and only on the port side of the ship.

"Side cannons one and three just fired," Stefan said, "but the rest aren't responding."

"Try again." Ruby turned. "Natasha, any luck re-routing us?"

"I'm getting *some* drift, but not enough. I just don't understand what's—"

The ship rocked again. But it was different this time: not one of the huge explosions that had shaken the Pantheon up to yet, but something smaller and more contained. It didn't come from the ship's side, either, but almost directly overhead.

"What—" Ruby started, but Amelie was already shouting:

"The porthole has been blown apart! We're open to attack!"

The cacophony frenzied. Ruby ordered the ship into lockdown, then shouted into her communicator before she'd even heard Sia's response. "Mikhail! Forget loading the cannons—I need you guys kitted out and upstairs. Bastards have just blown our porthole open."

His response was brief: "Aye."

Ruby looked around. Fingers were frenetic on keyboards, screens cycled through alerts and schematics and diagnostics. Amber and red text flashed everywhere. The faces behind the workstations were strained—scared.

By the door: Francis. He looked just as terrified as the others. Just as terrified as Ruby herself felt under this onslaught of fire and failing systems.

But then, he'd looked scared before, too. When he led an assassin right up to her door.

Fuming, Ruby crossed the floor to him. Trove stood to attention, but she ignored the man. Now her eyes sought Francis's: black seeking out whites.

"What's happening?" Francis breathed.

"You have to ask?" Ruby's tone was acid. "We're about to be *boarded*, Francis Paige. *Again*."

2

Francis stared, dumbfounded, at Ruby's blazing eyes.

"I—what—"

"Don't pretend you don't know what I'm saying," Ruby growled. She took a step closer and jabbed Francis in the chest. She was shorter than him by an inch, but that jab packed a lot of punch. "All this started after we picked up *you* from the *Eden*."

"Whoa, whoa!" That was Natasha. She hurried across the room. "Don't start attacking Francis! This isn't his fault!"

"No, of course not!" Ruby whirled, threw her arms in the air. "Because you vouched for him. And that means he's okay, right? That means he's not some kind of spy dumped here by that fucking Rhod Stein—"

If it could fall any further, Francis's mouth did then. "That's what you think?"

"*Yes, that's what I think!*" Ruby roared. "I've captained this ship for years, and in the couple of weeks since we picked up you, we've come under attack *three times*. Funny, wouldn't you say?"

"I didn't—"

"And then you start crawling around the ship all the time. I saw you the other morning, in the pantry."

"Getting supplies for breakfast!"

"Or poking around. Maybe you were learning more about the ship and its ins and outs after your first attempt on my life failed!"

"No!"

"And now you've gathered your information, we're under attack again! Or is that just a convenient coincidence?"

"Yes!"

Ruby looked ready to scream. "Don't you give me that—"

Natasha pushed between them. "Leave him alone!" She faced Ruby's crimson face. "Francis did *not* do this!"

"And how do you know? How can you profess to know his character so damn well?"

"Because I *talked to him*!" Natasha shouted. "I spent time with him! I tried to be there for him! I *empathised* with him, instead of thrusting a sword upon him and telling him to board a ship! Because unlike you, Ruby, I tried my best to understand what he was going through and his feelings, instead of trying to push him into the kinds of things *you* find exciting but *he* doesn't!"

There was silence. *Real* silence, Francis realised: everyone was listening. No hands on keyboards. Even the alarms had been quieted. Workstations sat forgotten as their technicians watched the drama unfolding by the open doorway.

"That's bullshit," Ruby said at last.

"No, it's not," said Natasha. "I may not have known him long, but I do know that this—these attacks—are *not* something Francis is capable of. He's a good person. *Like us.*"

If Ruby had a retort to that, it didn't come. Her radio clicked. With a begrudging look at Natasha and then Francis, she turned toward the centre of the room and lifted the communicator to her lips.

"Yes, Mikhail."

His voice came back, very slightly tinny: "We're in the corridor now, Captain."

"Anything?"

"Looks like they blew a pretty big hole in the roof. Porthole's gone, and the top of the ladder is a mess. But it's clear, and—wait—shit, guys, move!"

Cracks echoed over the link. Even over the communicator they were clear: gunshots.

"What's happening?"

Mikhail's voice was pocked by more gunshots. "Three of them! Just dropped down the—" Four fast shots, louder than the others, and then Mikhail was back. "Just took out one, but—"

Someone screamed in the background.

"Reuben!" Mikhail yelled.

"*What happened?*" Ruby shouted.

"Bullet to the leg—"

CRACK!

"They're pushing forward—"

CRACK!

"Don't know—"

There was a scuffle, a heavy sound very close by—then silence.

Ruby stared at her communicator in horror. All the colour drained from her face. "Mikhail?"

A voice answered, but it wasn't Mikhail's. Wasn't the voice of anyone on the ship at all.

"Hello, Ruby Celeste." A man: silky and dangerous. Like the one who'd held Francis at gunpoint. "I hoped I'd get to speak to you."

3

Tracking down the Pantheon had taken days.

The first time had been relatively simple. But after Miles had got himself killed, the Pantheon had fled and changed course. So what could have been a quick search had stretched into almost a week.

A week to mull things over.

Four men made up Imelda's collection of assassins. They were good—very good. Most of the operations were simple affairs; the men and women with money—the men and women whose last moments these four men all watched—were also men and women without any kind of ability when it came to self-defense. A few punches, maybe a fractured rib, but never anything that took too long to mend.

And then this Ruby Celeste woman. Another job from Rhod Stein, which was handed to Miles. Miles had tracked the ship, boarded, and then promptly vanished. Had to be dead. His Pod was abandoned, drifting.

Leon had found it.

Found his brother's empty ship.

He'd wailed at first. One hour, maybe two, just sat in that tiny craft, bawling to himself. His brain went through memories, tiny things he'd forgotten until now, like the time their parents had brought them to an arcade and Leon had run out of money. Always the same; the neon colours and jingling sounds unleashed the reckless gambler inside him, and before fifteen minutes had passed he'd cycled through as many machines as his allowance would permit. Then, near the back, he'd spied a grabber machine, and inside, at the very top, was a plush toy of his favourite comic book character. Leon just *had* to have it. But when he reached for a coin, he came up empty. The last had gone into a shoot-em-up game he'd barely lasted more than a minute at.

Faced with this object of his dreams (temporarily, anyway; before this morning it hadn't crossed his mind, and by next week would be forgotten) and no way of retrieving it, Leon did the only thing his young mind could think of: he began to cry.

Miles had heard. Miles was always more careful with money—with everything, really—and headed over, his pockets still jangling, to see what his younger brother was sobbing about. And then he popped one of his own coins into the machine, expertly (for an eight-year-old) worked the joystick, and ten seconds later out popped the plushie.

Memories like that. Little things that hadn't entered Leon's mind for years. Now they came back in a flood, each one bringing a stab of pain worse than the last.

Once his tears eventually petered out, he called Imelda. Like him, she was upset, though in perhaps a different way. Leon felt like he'd been gutted; Imelda was simply angry. Leon wasn't angry yet, but would be.

For now Imelda told him to leave things with her, and to tether the pod back. Later she would give instructions; just had to speak to Rhod first.

After she'd spoken to Stein, Imelda called her other two men back: Karl, built thick with a buzz cut, and a short, lithe fellow who had been introduced as Zed. Leon had a feeling that wasn't his real name, but the man was good—even more so considering he was approaching middle age—and thus he'd never questioned it.

The remaining trio were sent in search of the Pantheon. The assassination of this woman was in their hands now; it was just a matter of finding her.

A week of inaction was enough for Leon to grow inward. At first he'd simply been sad that his brother had been taken from him. But then, as the days lengthened and the Pantheon remained elusive, that sadness shifted into hate. Because *she* had done this: that woman on the ship they were searching for. Ruby Celeste had killed Miles.

So it would be Leon that killed Ruby. And he would enjoy it, too.

Zed had finally found the Pantheon, late last night. He had radioed Imelda, and then Leon and Karl; the three had returned to base, where they swapped their Pods for a sleek black craft. Long, it housed a lone cannon. Like the Pods, it also was home to a Volum, as well as eight supercharged batteries to deliver terrific speed. Still, those batteries wouldn't last: they'd catch up to the Pantheon, take her out, and have just enough juice left to get home before they were down to the Volum alone.

"Do not open fire," Imelda had warned as the men boarded. "Treat this as a normal operation. The cannon is only an option if she spots you first."

Leon planned to take that advice. But then, as they caught up with the ship this evening and radioed Imelda, he changed his mind.

"She's in our sights," he said.

"Good," was Imelda's answer. For all the distance, it was practically as though she was in the room. Expensive stuff, this tech, but Imelda was connected.

"Hanging pretty low."

"Just get above her and board. You know what to do after that."

Leon nodded. He was about to agree, but … something in him flexed. That woman in there had killed his brother. She was obviously cunning. And Leon wanted to make her hurt before he struck the head from her shoulders and torched the ship.

But boarding? Sneaking in and killing her, then setting the ship ablaze? That wasn't nearly good enough vengeance.

So he said, "No."

Karl and Zed looked around.

Imelda: "What?"

"I'm opening fire."

"No! That'll warn her!"

"Then it'll make it more *fun*."

"Don't you dare—"

But Imelda's words were lost as Leon cut the connection.

Karl and Zed looked at him expectantly. He gave them little

more than a glance before cycling through to the cannon controls and getting a lock on the ship.

Everything after that had been a blur. Instead of heading down and opening the porthole from the outside, Leon had smashed it open. For the best, really: some of these ships were outfitted with automated locking sequences that started up in case of attack. Now they'd bypassed that entirely.

All three had dropped in, and immediately met four men armed with pistols. A firefight erupted in the corridor. Quarters were tight; Karl took a bullet to the head and went down. Then Zed hit one of the Pantheon's men in the leg and knocked him out too. A few more shots had been squeezed off from either side, but the injured man had the crew's attention, and Leon had been able to stride over and knock out the big, black-haired fellow talking on his communicator. Zed had already dropped the other two.

And now here they were: stood inside this woman's ship, this *murderer's* ship, in a corridor pocked with bullet holes. And Leon was speaking to Celeste herself on this communicator.

"Who are you?" she demanded. There was ice in her voice, and she sounded young. Or maybe that was fear. An undercurrent, masked, but there. Celeste was scared. Good.

"That's irrelevant. For now. We've knocked out your men and confiscated their weapons. One of them has been shot, but I think he'll survive. Maybe."

"If you—"

"They're safe," said Leon. These situations were always the same. People were so predictable. "For now. But they won't be unless you come to us—*alone.*"

Silence. Leon waited, exchanging a look with Zed, and then pressed down on the communicator again. "I'll give you two minutes. If you don't show up alone, and unarmed, I will shoot one of these men. Every sixty seconds that pass, another will die. And once all four are gone, I'm coming for you. Understand me?"

Celeste's voice came back, flat. "Yes."

"Good. I'll start counting, then."

Leon switched off the communicator, dropped it to the floor. It had been handy, if a little rusted.

Now it was just a question of waiting.

4

All eyes were on Ruby. Ten seconds passed as she stood silently, eyes boring somewhere through the floor.

"Ruby," Natasha started.

The Pantheon's captain turned and headed for the door. Natasha stepped into her path and grabbed her by the shoulders.

"What are you doing?"

"You heard the man," Ruby said. "I've got two minutes. One hundred and twenty seconds. Probably about ninety now. I need to go."

"But they'll kill you—"

"And they'll kill four of my crew if I don't." Ruby inhaled. "Natasha Brady, I am ordering you to stand aside. Same for the rest of you by the door. Trove. And you, Francis."

"Ruby—"

"That's an *order*, Natasha. I am your captain. Now move."

Francis thought she wouldn't, *wished* she wouldn't. But Natasha did step aside, as did Trove, and Ruby strode toward the door.

"Your sword," Natasha called as Ruby passed over the threshold. "They want you to go unarmed."

"That's correct; they do."

And then Ruby was gone.

5

Exactly twenty seconds remained when a woman appeared at the end of the corridor. A short woman with crimson curls underneath a ridiculous tricorne hat.

"So," Leon said. "You must be Ruby Celeste."

She waited. Her at one end, the two men at the other, a bundle of four unconscious bodies behind. There was blood, too, smeared across the floor where someone had been dragged. That was Evans. Ruby assessed without even looking at it. Scarlet and unsightly, but not too much. He wasn't bleeding out. That was good. Stitches. If he got out of this.

Ruby said, "I am. And would you care to explain who you are?"

6

"No," Zed answered, but Leon stepped in front of him at the same moment and said, "You killed my brother." He levelled his gun at Ruby's head. One shot. One squeeze of the trigger. It was so tempting now they were face to face.

Ruby looked from Leon to Zed and back again. "Sounds like that one speaks for you," she said. Her tone was cold, unflinching.

Leon took another step, jabbed at the air. Four metres of clearance between them, easy. But still she wasn't threatened. Or if she was, she wasn't showing it.

"Maybe you should be quiet and let him do the talking," Ruby said. "You're clearly agitated."

"You killed my brother!"

"Did I." It wasn't a question. There wasn't even the slightest hint of interest to her voice. Celeste just sounded *bored*.

Heat rose in Leon's stomach. Another step. Behind him, Zed warned, "Leon."

"Yes, Ruby Celeste, you did. So now I'm going to kill you. But I'm going to make it hurt. Do you understand that?" She didn't answer, so Leon jabbed the gun again. Maybe even shortened their gap further. He wasn't sure. "I said, do you understand that?"

"I'll tell you what I understand," said Ruby. Now *she* moved forward. It was small, a half-step, but enough for Zed to say something. Some warning, some word; yet it was lost. "You opened fire on my ship. Destroyed our navigational control, took out our cameras. Blew a hole in it. Shot at my men—injured one of them.

"Yes, I did kill your brother. The guy that appeared last week, right? I know the one. Blew his brains out myself. Splattered them over the wall. He tried to get a shot off, but clearly I'm just too quick."

Boiling blood coursed Leon's veins. His hand shook. Ruby was closer now, had inched further up the corridor, he was sure. Almost close enough to reach out and grab, to wrap his hands around, to scream in her face as it went crimson, then purple, then blue ...

"You're wrong," Ruby continued in a low, dangerous voice. Her eyes flashed. "You will not hurt me; not you, nor the man behind you."

"And why's that?" Leon hissed.

"Because you don't have a gun."

And before another word could leave Leon's throat, or before the warning escaped Zed's, she reached for the sword sheathed at her waist, drew it, and sliced Leon's arm off at the wrist in one smooth, clean motion.

7

A bullet whizzed up the corridor and embedded itself in the wall where Ruby had been standing a moment ago. But she was safe: she'd positioned herself just enough behind this angry man that the other assailant couldn't get a killing shot off if he tried. Not unless he wanted to kill the person he'd come here with.

The man was screaming even before his severed forearm hit the ground. The gun went off, blowing up splinters inches from Ruby's feet. Blood pounded out in a hot river. He clutched the stump, but his fingers did nothing to stem the flow.

Another gunshot, and this time Ruby felt the fabric of her jacket rip.

Quickly, she thought. This guy was out of action, but the other was too far away. She couldn't get to him without making herself a perfect target. Even if she didn't move, he only needed to straighten his aim just a little more …

She stooped, snatched the gun up in her left hand.

Springing to one side, she took aim. Another gun pointed back at her.

She fired.

The bullet struck him in the stomach. He fell backward, squeezing his own trigger, burying a bullet in the ceiling. Clattering; the gun fell from his hand.

"Now," Ruby said. She tossed her pistol away and rounded on the first man. He was pressed up against the wall, burbling incoherently. His face was papery and white. "I don't know who you are, or why you're here …"

"Please," he wheezed. "Pl-please …"

"But you attacked my ship, and my people. And you will *never*—" she swung the sword up high; he screamed "—*do*—" down it sailed, embedding deep into his neck; the wail turned into a gurgle; his eyes bulged "—*that*—" another swing, another strike; claret sailed "—*AGAIN!*"

The final blow split him right down the middle. His husk slumped sideways. Panting, Ruby yanked the sword free. The blade was slick, coated in maroon. As was the hallway. As was Ruby.

Her chest heaved.

Then there was a gunshot, and wood exploded behind her. She yelped, stumbled backward. The sword fell from her grasp.

The other man: leaned back against the wall, clothes rapidly soaking in his own blood. But he was alive, and he stared at Ruby down the barrel of his reclaimed pistol. Empty space between them: no cover, and with her gun and sword lost, no weapons, either.

She was cornered.

8

"We can't just leave her by herself!"

That was Natasha.

The control room was torn. There were two options: go after Ruby—or stay away.

"You heard the man on the radio," Stefan countered. "If she doesn't go up alone, Mikhail and the others will die!"

"She was supposed to go unarmed and didn't do that," said Natasha. "How do we know they're not dead already?"

"Because we haven't heard gunshots."

"Who says they've only got guns?"

"Who else besides our captain carries a sword?"

"That man who boarded us last week had a dagger!" Natasha looked around the room at the faces staring back at her. All scared, all with no idea what to do. "Come on, we can't just leave her! She's outnumbered!"

"She's smart," Trove said. "And Stefan is right: you heard the man on the radio. If anyone else goes up there, four innocent men will die."

"Our *captain* will die! Isn't anyone going to think about that?"

Quiet. No one wanted to speak.

Then at last, one voice made itself heard: Francis.

"She's right," he said. "Mikhail said there were three men, and one got taken out. So that leaves two. Ruby—she's got a sword. If we could go up there with a gun, we could … could tip the odds in her favour. *Our* favour." His eyes roved from person to person. "Evans already got shot. We could stop it from happening to anyone else."

Again, silence. Natasha waited. "*Well?*" she pleaded.

A crack rung out on the level above. Another followed, then a third.

And then silence.

"That's it," Natasha said. She stormed to Trove, who stood blocking the door. "You can complain all you want, but you're not going to stop me leaving."

He might have fought, but the gunshots had turned his skin another shade of white. Instead he simply nodded, and stepped sideways so Natasha could pass.

She didn't move. "I want your gun."

She reached into his jacket and withdrew it. Somewhat oversized, it looked too big in her hands; she was daintier than Trove, even if she did match his height inch for inch. Natasha looked the weapon over, checked it was loaded, and then gave one final glance at the faces in the room.

"Stay safe."

Then she, too, was out the door.

Halfway up the hallway, a voice called her name. She turned, keeping the pistol aimed at the floor.

Francis bounded up behind her.

"What are you doing?" she asked.

"What does it look like? I'm coming with you."

Natasha gaped. "You're not armed."

"I know," Francis said with a grimace. "But maybe I can be a distraction. Now come on."

He overtook, pushing up the corridor, and Natasha had no choice but to follow.

9

Here Ruby was, trapped: no weapon, no cover, and the man across from her had a clear shot.

So this is it, she thought. *This is how I'm going to die.*

She only prayed that he bled out before turning on the rest of the crew. Her life to save the others. It was an even trade, she thought.

Footsteps clattered up the corridor. More than one pair. What was going on? Had more men boarded the ship before Mikhail and the others arrived to head them off? Was the Pantheon overrun?

"Hey!"

That was a man's voice—a voice Ruby recognised. She dared

look back. There, bursting around the corner, was Francis, arms above his head in a manic wave.

"Hey! I'm Francis Paige, the 'stolen property'! It's me you're looking for!"

Ruby gaped. "Francis?"

The next two seconds were the longest of her life.

She swivelled back to the bleeding man. Shifting his contorted features to Francis, he swung the gun to track Paige's footsteps hurtling up the corridor.

Another voice shouted, "Now!"

Francis dived. Behind him, squatted at the end of the hallway, a great pistol in her hands—Trove's pistol, Ruby was sure of it—was Natasha, her face set.

The navigation leader pulled the trigger.

At what seemed like the same instant, but couldn't have been, surely not, the bleeding man squeezed his own.

Searing, white hot pain exploded in Ruby's side. The impact tossed her backward, and she hit the wall lopsided before crashing into a heap.

10

Francis picked himself up from the floor. He'd hit his head—that was twice in less than twenty minutes now—and his vision spun. His brain felt completely shaken, because as he struggled to stand he couldn't be sure if there had been one gunshot or two. It sounded like one, but some part of him was sure that wasn't right.

Natasha flew up the corridor. She passed Francis, and he stumbled to avoid her. Something wet underfoot almost took his legs out from under him, but he pressed a steadying hand to the wall. He looked down to see what the slick was.

Blood. Lots of it. It practically coated the corridor. How hadn't he seen it before? Oh, yes, that was it: he had sprinted toward an armed man to help save a woman who, moments ago, had accused Francis of luring these attackers here.

"Francis! Francis, I need you!"

Blinking hard, he looked to where Natasha crouched by Ruby's still form.

He rushed forward, stepping over Ruby's bloodied sword, and stooped by the captain. Her clothes were red, soaked; her face stained, as if her hair had liquefied and was running down it in crimson rivulets. This couldn't all be her blood, could it? Otherwise how had she been standing?

No, it wasn't. Because up ahead, the bleeding man—dead man, now, half of his face missing—had lost his own fair share. Behind him, a cluster of unconscious bodies. One of those was bleeding, too. And what was that husk of a thing Francis had run by just now? That meaty sack of gore he'd seen but not taken in, not until now, when he was sat just inches from it.

He closed his eyes, breathed deep. Iron hung in the air, he was sure of it. Cloying, sickening, it worked into the back of his throat.

"Francis, don't grey out on me!"

Natasha's voice seemed to come from a long way off. Focussing hard, Francis pushed his way out of the fog. His eyes flickered open.

Relief crossed Natasha's face for just a second. "Good, you're okay. I need you to help me, all right? Ruby—she's bleeding. We need to get her to Darrel. Evans, too."

Francis nodded. His eyes drifted down to Ruby. A hole was ripped in the side of her jacket. The shirt beneath had been white, but now it was stained red. He whimpered and looked away.

"I don't like blood," he said.

"I know you don't," Natasha answered. "And you're doing great, really great. I'm going to handle this, but I need you to radio the others—Darrel, then Trove. With my communicator, okay?" She yanked it off and thrust it at him; then she grabbed Ruby's jacket and ripped, widening the maw. "I need to try to stop the bleeding, so I can't. Can you do that?"

His voice wavered. "I don't know how it works."

"It's okay, just listen to me and I'll tell you." Panic rose even higher in Natasha's voice, and Francis averted his eyes as Ruby's stomach came into view. Too late: there was a puncture right at the edge, where her body curved away.

"Will she—"

"Francis! I need you to concentrate!"

Francis breathed deep. Looked at Natasha's face. Had to: if he looked anywhere else he was sure he would pass out. "Okay. Tell me what to do."

"Press the star button to switch on the display."

Francis pressed it. His fingers quivered, almost missed, but he managed. "Okay."

"There's a little menu. Use the arrows to cycle through to contacts." She waited a second. "Done that?"

"Y-yeah."

"Okay. Almost there. It's simple, see? Now use the arrows again to cycle through to Darrel. Darrel Stitt. Only one under D. Found him?"

"Got him."

"Okay, now press the green button twice. You lift it and speak into it, all right?"

"Yeah. I—I've seen people do it."

For two seconds there was only silence—no, not silence, but Natasha as she panted and tore the sleeve from her own jacket and pressed it to Ruby's wound. Then a click, and a voice.

"Natasha?"

"Err, no," said Francis shakily. "It's Francis—Francis Paige. Um—you're the doctor here, right?"

"Miss Celeste is injured up here!" Natasha shouted. "Took a bullet to the abdomen! I need you to be prepared to fix her!"

"I—okay!" Darrel called back. "But the office is in lockdown— I'm stuck inside. I can't do anything until it's lifted."

"That's okay; just prepare a bed!"

"Or two," Francis added. "Evans got shot as well."

Darrel: "Oh God … Is Miss Celeste's condition serious?"

Suddenly, Ruby's body spasmed. She coughed. Natasha half-fell backward, and Francis stared in terror. Were these death throes?

But the captain's eyes flickered open and her coughs petered out. Her eyes moved between Francis and Natasha and back again, before falling to the communicator Francis held. She extended a limp hand and took it from him.

"I'll live," she rasped. "Don't think it—hit anything—" Her eyes swum back up to Natasha. Normally blue, they'd taken on a watery, dull colour. Behind all the spatters of claret, her face was ghost-like. "These guys rescued me." A weary glance to Francis. Her hand was dropping as her strength faded out. "I'll call Sia; get lockdown lifted. See you in five, Darrel."

"Okay."

Natasha reached for the communicator. "I'll do that."

"No. Just—stop me bleeding."

No argument. Natasha nodded and pressed hard on Ruby's abdomen again. Ruby grimaced and drew a sharp intake of breath. She said, "Francis– I need you to—do the buttons."

He reached out. "Okay." Called.

Trove answered. "Miss Brady?"

"It's Ruby."

"Miss Celeste! Are you—you sound—"

"Ssh," Ruby said. Her hand drooped; Francis held it steady. "End the lockdown. Then come up—help bring me to—Darrel—"

She fell silent and her eyes closed.

Natasha gasped. "Is she …"

Francis pressed his fingers into her neck, just below her jawline. It was sticky with blood, but he blocked it out.

"She's alive," he answered. "There's a pulse. Must have just passed out." He lifted the communicator and held it by his mouth. "Trove, it's Francis. You heard her. Get the ship out of lockdown, then get whoever you can to help. Ruby needs to get to Darrel. She's bleeding. I—I don't know how long …"

"Okay," said Trove. "I'm on it."

Francis looked at Natasha. Still she pressed on the wound.

Though the material of her jacket was black, it seemed somehow blacker against Ruby's stomach—soaking with her blood.

"Anyone else I should call?"

"No. That's it."

The communicator fell from Francis's hands with a dull thud. Both ignored it.

"Will she …"

Natasha: "Yes." Her voice was firm. "Yes, she'll live. She damn well has to."

11

Ruby would live, it turned out. The bullet had punctured her midsection, but only the very side; it had torn some muscle, but hit nothing life-threatening. Still, it would put her out of action for some time as she recovered from the ordeal.

Evans would live too. In fact, he was up and at it again by lunch the following day. Hobbling around on a crutch, he did his best to laugh and joke—but it was tough. It was clear from his face he was just as strained as the rest of them.

And no wonder. The Pantheon was a wreck. An enormous hole ripped in the top, the outer hull almost destroyed, no working cameras, a failing control centre, one fin missing, minimal navigational control, a Volum that clearly had something wrong, rust eating its way through the lower portion of the ship, *and* no captain. They were in dire straits, and everyone knew it.

Cacophonous Harmonics was a day and a half away. Natasha had managed to push the ship onto the correct course—barely—so they would stop there. It was just a case of managing to sustain this hobbling lurch.

The Explosive Rage of Rhod Stein

(Chapter Fifteen)

1

After a full night without sleep, Rhod should have been tired. But he wasn't. Instead he was operating on a mix of coffee and the antsy feeling he'd harboured in his stomach since Imelda's call yesterday.

The attack had been last night; standard. Imelda would know how it had gone down already, but maybe she was doing this to toy with him. Oh, how that woman loved to toy with him. Twice Rhod had thought about calling her. But he'd decided to wait. There was no badgering Imelda; she would just be infuriating and withhold information until he was willing to be 'patient'. Willing to be strung along, more like. Still: he waited.

It was approaching noon now, and he downed the morning's fourth mug of coffee. Bitter, horrid stuff, but it helped. It saw him through the night after his anticipation alone wasn't enough; now it would see him through until Imelda's call finally came.

Waiting was a dull game. Worse than that, it bred concerns, worries; let the mind go off with itself and spin stories of how things might have gone wrong.

But it couldn't have. This time Imelda had sent in *all* of her men—or those remaining, at least. One man could fail, but a trio? They would surely have cornered Celeste, hacked her screaming head from her shoulders. A head that would soon be mounted like a trophy upon the wall of Rhod's new office, when *The Pharmacologist's Eden* was rebuilt and open once more. Maybe he would make it even more fantastic, more amazing, just to spite her. Her lifeless eyes could look down upon it for eternity, staring at what she'd tried to destroy but Rhod had reconstructed, bigger, better than before.

The phone rang. Rhod snatched it up even before the first trill silenced. His heart, already speeding from the vast amounts of caffeine, raced faster. Adrenaline surged, turning his fingertips hot.

"Yes?"

"Rhod."

"Did you get her?"

There was an infuriating moment of quiet; toying with him again, stirring him up so she could get a rise out of him—and then Imelda's voice came back. "No. No, we didn't. They didn't."

Heat was replaced by ice in Rhod's veins. His vision tunnelled. They'd failed? Was this a joke? Some cruel jape?

No. It wasn't. He could tell by Imelda's voice. For the first time she sounded flat—defeated. There was no smugness, no smarminess to her words, none of that silkiness Rhod hated so much. Now she just sounded *old*.

"What?" he whispered.

"They opened fire on her ship. I told them not to, but Leon cut me off. I didn't hear from them after that. Haven't heard from them since."

"Could they be … could Celeste have captured them?"

"No," was Imelda's glum answer. "Well. Could have. But I don't think so, do you?"

Rhod's mind whirled. Twice now Imelda had failed. Twice the Pantheon had been boarded, and twice the boarders had been bested by that damn crimson-haired woman. A woman who had shattered the empire he'd built and was now staving off everything Rhod threw at her while his money pissed out of his pockets.

"*God damn it!*" he exploded. "*Damn you! Why can't you do a simple fucking job?*"

"We tried. She must be experienced, or—"

"It was a SIMPLE TASK! BOARD HER SHIP, BRING ME BACK HER HEAD AND TORCH THE REST! I've fed you money for the past week and a half while your men track her down, and for what? Nothing but wasted time!"

"Rhod—"

"Rhod nothing! This is the last time I will EVER work with you, you useless, good-for-nothing old WITCH!"

With a roar, he slammed the phone down into its cradle, tore it from the wall, and smashed it to pieces.

He shuddered with racking, angered breaths.

Ruby Celeste was still out there.

Well, maybe Rhod could do what Imelda's goons hadn't been able to. And he'd be able to enjoy it more, too. All it took was finding the woman—and Imelda had already told him where she was: heading toward a little SkyPort called *Cacophonous Harmonics.*

2

Rhod flew from the makeshift office in a rage. All around, *The Pharmacologist's Eden* was heaving. At long last, the first new buildings were starting to take shape.

It no longer seemed very important.

He stormed across the open plaza, heading straight for the first stairway to the parking bay.

Behind him, someone called, "Mr Stein?" When Rhod didn't turn, he called louder, "Mr Stein?"

Rhod spun. "*What?*"

It was Lance; that damned know-nothing who'd kept the *Eden* closed all this time. Lance looked pleased, for some reason: probably the thrill of seeing Rhod in a raging mood. Well, Rhod would show him. He thundered toward the man.

"I just wanted to give you an update," Lance started.

He didn't get to finish. As Rhod brought the gap between them to little more than a metre, he drew his pistol from his belt, levelled it and fired. There was a spray of crimson, and Lance hit the floor.

In the wake of the crack, silence reigned. Heads turned, horrified. To one side gaped Lars and Charlotte. Damn couples.

Rhod gave his watchers little more than a glance. "Someone clean this up!" he ordered. Then he turned tail and continued his march to the parking bay, and with it, his ship.

3

Rhod's ship was custom-built for one, yet so large it looked as if it could house at least a dozen. And no wonder: he demanded a kick out of it, so four Volum occupied it in a cluster toward the rear, along with another four supercharged batteries. It was a hulking behemoth of machine; inside was just one room and one corridor, plus a minute storage bay.

Long, sleek and black, it began as a point, widened and then blossomed at the back in a flower-like arrangement of bulbs that held the Volum. A single cannon ran from end to end; no side cannons, but there was no need. The entire ship was coated in a thin layer of material to direct thrust: Rhod had unequalled turning speed and fidelity. If he needed to realign for a shot, he could do so. Not that he planned on opening fire on the Pantheon.

Well. Maybe just once.

Rhod climbed in via side door, headed down the corridor and into the control room. An arc-shaped console spread out in front of the viewing screen, a plush chair bolted down underneath. Rhod hefted into it, then brought his systems online. The computer asked him where he wanted to go, and he answered, "*Cacophonous Harmonics.*" It paused to evaluate what he'd said, and a moment later updated the display to show an image of the SkyPort, plus travel time. From here, a little over twenty-four hours.

"Well then," Rhod said. "Let's go."

Without much more than a very low noise, Rhod's ship pulled

out of the parking bay. It reoriented itself, moving in a small curve to point straight for its destination. And then it began to move; slowly at first, but picking up speed with every second.

On screen, the timer ticked down. When it reached zero, Rhod would find Celeste—and his revenge would be had.

Cacophonous Harmonics
(Chapter Sixteen)

1

For the past twenty-four hours, a low feeling of tension had pervaded the Pantheon's crew. Finally they were on the last stretch of the trek to *Cacophonous Harmonics*. Due to arrive sometime soon, that tension had fizzled out until it was replaced by relief: relief that, at long last, they were almost safe.

Regular tasks on the Pantheon had been interrupted. The workhands were without work—no sense maintaining a ship on the verge of falling apart—while the ship's technicians had long since given up attempting to get their computer systems working normally again. Now most of the crew were milling about, some in their quarters, some in the library or rec room. For Francis, the place to be was the control room: Natasha was there, slumped over her workstation, along with Mikhail, who had taken up Stefan's vacant seat.

"Won't be long now," Natasha mumbled.

Francis nodded.

"Afternoon, troops."

Their heads all swung to the doorway at once. Entering at a hobble, a swath of bandages wrapped around her midriff, was Ruby.

"Miss Celeste!" Natasha cried. She was up on her feet immediately. Ruby waved her off and dropped down into the closest seat. "You shouldn't be up and about in your condition."

"I'm fine, I'm fine." Her eyes looked over the screen in front of her, but it was garbled. She surveyed the few in the room, eyes falling last to Francis and then dropping to the floor. "Status report?"

"Did Darrel let you leave?"

"Easy, Natasha," Ruby said. "No, he didn't, but I gave him an order and he was unable to refuse."

Natasha was no more pacified by that, but sat back into her seat regardless, her face drawn tight.

"Now," Ruby went on, "status report?"

"Most systems still offline," said Amelie. "I can give you a blow-by-blow account …"

"That won't be necessary. How close are we to port?"

"Not sure; with cameras offline, we're performing visual checks. Should be there soon, though."

"Speaking of," Natasha said. She pushed up onto her feet and headed for the door. "I'd best go do one. See you shortly."

Ruby rearranged herself in the seat, slowly. A distinctly pained expression crossed her face as she moved. Then she looked up, met Francis's eyes. Her mouth worked.

Trove stepped through the door. "Miss Celeste! Darrel just informed me—"

"Yes, yes, I've had it all already," Ruby said wearily. "Take a seat. I'm waiting for Natasha's report on our progress."

Trove sat down, looking discomfited. "I really think," he began, but Ruby shot him a tired look and he silenced.

The wait for Natasha's radio call was quiet, but short. Thirty seconds later Amelie's communicator clicked.

"Hey, Amelie. Looks like we're almost there. I can see the port up ahead; half a mile away at most. Parking bays are pretty empty, so should be simple enough to pull up. I'll stay on deck to direct."

"Excellent."

"There's another ship out here," Natasha said. "I guess that's heading for *Harmonics* too. I'll keep an eye on it, make sure we give it a wide berth."

"Great." Amelie's screen cycled through to the navigation

controls. The display flickered precariously, but held. "Awaiting further instructions."

Francis sat forward in his chair. At last, after what felt like weeks, they were inches from victory. The ship would be repaired. Francis would get to see if someone might know a way he could get home. And whatever happened with him, the crew would get some time out, too. A godsend after this past fortnight.

Something beeped; a noise Francis didn't recognise.

"Err, Miss Celeste?" said Amelie. "We're being hailed."

"Patch it through."

Amelie entered a string of commands. "It should be connected. Assuming—"

She was cut off by the booming, bark-like voice that blared from the speakers.

"I demand to speak to Ruby Celeste!"

Curious faces turned to Ruby. She looked just as confused as the rest of them. Picking herself up, she half-limped to Amelie's station. Amelie evacuated the seat, and Ruby took it.

"This is she. Who am I speaking to?"

"Aha. *Ruby Celeste*. It was only a matter of time before I caught up to you." The man laughed, a sneering and unpleasant noise. The speakers warbled and then cut off the transmission. Ruby jabbed at the keyboard. Something worked: the noise ceased and was replaced by that brutish voice:

"—made a laughing stock out of me, Celeste. And *nobody* makes a laughing stock out of me."

More harshly, Ruby repeated, "Who am I speaking to?"

"*Rhod Stein!* Remember? You *stole* from me, blew a hole in my SkyPort, and then killed *every single man* I sent to bring me your head on a stick!"

Francis glanced about the room. Tension choked the atmosphere again. Mikhail looked fraught. Wheels turned behind his eyes.

"Natasha," he mumbled.

"So the old adage is true," Rhod went on. "If you want something doing, you have to do it yourself."

Mikhail jerked up and crossed the room in three long strides. "Natasha," he repeated, more urgently. "She's on deck. She's—"

"By the way, Celeste: your ship is looking awfully damaged. Won't you allow me to help?"

Ruby slammed the keyboard and cut the transmission, then spun to face Mikhail. "Hail her now!"

2

Up on the top deck, Natasha watched the diminutive SkyPort grow. In just a moment she would need to radio Amelie and give the final course corrections.

As she waited, she glanced backward at the other ship she'd seen. Black, bulbous to the rear, it appeared to have stopped, hovering some distance behind. Waiting for the Pantheon to park? Maybe; this ship was a state. The black vessel's pilot was probably just being considerate so as not to put any extra stress on the occupants of this wreck.

Her communicator clicked. An incoming transmission from Mikhail. "Yes?"

"Natasha! You need to come down from the deck!" His voice was frantic.

"What?"

"Get down! That other ship—it's Stein, and he's—"

Rhod!

Natasha looked up at the other ship, horror written over her features.

Then an explosion, and the world turned white.

3

"It's Stein, and he's about to open fire!"

Mikhail never finished the sentence. The Pantheon was rocked by the biggest explosion Francis had ever felt. He was flung from his seat and crashed into the wall. Pain exploded across his ribs.

And still the rumbling didn't end.

Alarms wailed, barely audible over the ringing in his ears.

When Francis opened his eyes again, the world was lopsided. The lights had gone off, replaced by a single flashing red beacon that painted the control centre the shade of a nightmare. And—had the opposite wall split apart?

"Natasha! What happened to Natasha?"

"I don't know! All I've got is static!"

Francis shoved onto his feet. The world should have evened out, but it didn't: this whole room was canted, one side higher than the rest. Wood panelling had split from the wall, and beneath was rusted metal, sheared apart.

"What's going on?" Francis said. Something creaked under him, and he slipped sideways and hit the wall. It was harder to right himself this time; every moment the world turned more on edge.

"*What's going on?*"

"Brace yourselves!" Ruby shouted. "I think we're going to crash!"

Francis gaped. "*Crash? Into what?*"

A rumble like no other shook the ship as it collided with *something—The SkyPort,* some working part of Francis's mind told him. Steel shrieked and tore: a bestial metal moan, wending through the Pantheon like a final agonised scream. The floor shook. Again, Francis careened into the wall. He held on desperately, but the room didn't stop turning; screams were buried by the noise as bodies slid past. One of the workstations disconnected, cables holding it for a moment before they too ripped apart, and then it smashed steel inches from where Francis was plastered. It tore open a rift and fell into the adjacent corridor.

This is it, Francis thought as his mouth screamed on autopilot and his terrified eyes trawled the room breaking into pieces all around him. *I'm going to die.*

4

Someone was helping him to his feet. He felt the world spin for a second—were they still crashing?—before a great pair of hands steadied him. He focussed: Mikhail. Behind was what had once been this room's floor; now a lopsided wall, not entirely solid. A thin sheet of smoke clung to the ceiling, snaking in through holes. Somewhere—maybe everywhere—the Pantheon was ablaze.

"What happened?" Francis gasped.

"We crashed into the SkyPort," Mikhail answered grimly. "And—Natasha—"

"She's out there." Ruby lifted herself from the bedraggled heap she'd landed in, with Trove's assistance. Her tricorne had been lost; she stooped and pulled it back onto askew hair. Blood trickled from the corner of her mouth. In the red light it looked nearer black than maroon.

"She was on deck when he attacked," said Mikhail.

"*She's out there,*" Ruby repeated.

"Miss Celeste …" Trove began.

"I said she's out there!" Ruby cried. Her eyes blazed. Shimmered. Her voice quaked. "I need you to find her."

Trove: "But …"

"*Find her!*" Tears spilled down Ruby's cheeks. She turned from her assistant to Mikhail, moved to him on unsteady feet. One hand gripped her bandaged side. "Mikhail, find Natasha Brady. That's an order."

He nodded. "Okay."

"Trove. Give the instruction to anyone that somehow missed the alarm. Get off the ship. Then help evacuate the SkyPort before the fire spreads."

Somewhere they heard a distant rumble. The floor shook again, and Francis clawed desperately at the nearest remaining workstation in case a maw opened and he was swallowed.

"Was that part of the ship?" Trove asked.

"Too far away," Mikhail said mutely. "*Harmonics,* maybe."

"We need to move." That was Ruby. She surveyed their faces. Wetness on her cheeks reflected the pulsing red light. "The ship is on fire. It's—it's falling to pieces." Her voice broke. She closed her eyes and stood a little taller as if that might hold the tears at bay. Trove moved to clasp her shoulder, but she brushed out of his grip. "Get out. All of you."

"And you, Miss Celeste," Trove said.

"I will. But I need to get something first."

"Then I'll—"

Ruby rounded on him. "You're not waiting with me!" she sobbed. "Get off this ship, all of you, and help evacuate the port! I'll catch up!"

Trove's face was ashen. He opened his mouth to argue, but Ruby cut across. "That's an *order*, Trove Wellbeing. Honour your captain's orders."

Finally, he nodded. Reluctantly: "As you wish. Stay safe, Miss Celeste." And without another word, he moved through a hole carved in the once-floor and disappeared.

Amelie, go."

"Yes, Miss Celeste. Stay safe."

Next, to Mikhail: "Find Natasha."

"On it. See you topside, Captain."

That just left Ruby and Francis. He watched. She had seemed so strong, infallibly brave—and here she stood across from him now, bleeding, clutching the wound at her side, her face stricken with tears.

"Go," she said at last. "With Mikhail. And find her."

"What about you?"

"I'll be fine."

"But the ship—"

"*I'll be fine.*" She stared as if begging him to believe her—and then she lifted her arm, the one gripping her bandage, and unhooked the communicator at her wrist. She tossed it to Francis; he caught it. "Take it. You know how they work. Liaise with the others."

"Ruby—"

"I'm giving you an order, Francis. You're part of my crew. So *go*."

He wanted to fight, really wanted to. But the others had tried and failed. He had no choice in the matter. So after a moment's struggle that seemed far longer, Francis gave a curt nod and headed out through the gap in the wall the same way the others had, leaving the Pantheon's captain alone in her ruined ship.

5

Watching the Pantheon crash into the SkyPort was, without question, the high point of Rhod's life. And it would only get better: that nefarious captain had a way of snaking out of danger; she'd escaped his clutches within his own SkyPort, making away with a deckhand, and then escaped assassination twice by Imelda's usually skilled men. So there was little doubt in Rhod's mind that she had somehow managed to survive the impact.

Which meant he would take the chase onto *Cacophonous Harmonics* itself.

Whereas *The Pharmacologist's Eden* was a sprawling burg of storefronts and plazas, *Cacophonous Harmonics* was much smaller. Less than a quarter the size of Rhod's empire, it was one level only, with a few dozen shops. The centre was open—well, mostly; now a wrecked ship occupied part of the space—and heaved with people. They were moving chaotically.

And no wonder, Rhod thought with a cruel smile.

Celeste would escape her ship, he was sure. Directly into chaos. But people dashing madly for the exits didn't make quite enough chaos to slow her down. It would only take a short run to the parking bay and a lifeboat, and then she would slip out of Rhod's clutches again.

So maybe he could tip the scales a little further in his favour.

The cannon reloaded, and he swivelled the ship so that it pointed directly at the port's opposite corner.

"Fire."

The world flashed with white as one corner of *Cacophonous Harmonics* disappeared. Debris rained in all directions, and fires flared. The chaos below intensified.

So. That was how it felt to attack a SkyPort. Perhaps it was something Rhod would try again sometime.

No time to think about that right now though. Rhod manoeuvred his craft and prepared to dock. It was time to find Ruby Celeste and exact revenge at last.

6

Escaping the ruined Pantheon alone might have been near impossible, but there were others fighting their way through the ship. Francis caught up with Vala and Stefan as they pushed through a corridor that was now too short to stand in; Vala wrapped him in a tight hug, Stefan clapped him on the shoulder, and they pressed through together, Francis following in their wake.

"Where's Ruby?" Vala asked.

"She's coming." At least, Francis hoped so. But he pushed the thought from his mind: first and foremost was finding Natasha. He would have to trust Ruby could take care of herself.

Stefan pulled at a sheet of metal. It held stiff, but then sheared away in one sudden movement. "Whoa!" he cried, backpedalling. Smoke poured out of the wound and plumed up the corridor. "Go back!"

They went back the way they'd come, arms pressed to mouths. The smoke had started as snaking tendrils, but continued to grow thicker. God damn it, why did so much of this ship have to be made of wood?

"This way!" Francis shouted. He pushed through a hole they'd gone past already. The squeeze was tight, and rusted metal tore open his shirt and scratched a crimson streak in his shoulder. He tamped down his gasp. "I think I can see light!"

A dim glow shone up ahead, barely more than a line: a rip in the outer hull? Francis worked toward it. He almost tripped, but Vala caught him, herself steadied by Stefan behind her.

"Thanks," he breathed.

"Don't mention it."

They reached the tear. Sure enough, the air smelled slightly fresher here, seeping in from outside. Francis ran his fingers around the opening in the metal. This was supposed to be several inches thick—would they ever get through?

"It's barely held together; we can do this. On three!" Stefan said. Francis and Vala nodded. "One, two, three!"

They rammed with their shoulders. It shuddered. They moved back, Stefan counted again, and hit it hard. This time it rocked, but held firm.

"One more should do it," he grunted. "Give it everything you've got. One, two, *three*!"

Francis threw every ounce of strength he had into the thrust. For an instant it seemed the hull would only rock beneath them, but then it tore clear and they tumbled out. Francis hung in the air for a moment, then crashed to the ground of the SkyPort, two metres below, Vala and Stefan landing beside him.

"Vala! Are you okay?" Stefan was already on his feet, pulling his wife up.

"Fine," she said. "Francis?"

"I'm okay," he mumbled. But he wasn't: his body groaned. Something had to be broken, he was sure of it.

"Can you get up?"

He rolled over. Blue sky swivelled into view. And the Pantheon—or what was left of it. Little more than two weeks ago, he'd seen this ship for the first time: majestic, sleek, and perfect, even if Natasha did say it was old. Now it was a ruin: a tangled mass of wood and metal, smoke pouring out of the many holes in its shattered carapace. It barely resembled a ship anymore.

He didn't get long to look. Vala and Stefan were already pulling him to his feet. The world swum, and he breathed hard to steady it before he greyed out. His hands were bloodied, he saw, and crimson speckled his vision.

"You're bleeding," said Vala.

"So are you," Francis retorted.

Cacophonous Harmonics was nothing compared to *The Pharmacologist's Eden*. Not least because it heaved with screaming shoppers, and flames were spreading very quickly from the far corner, incinerating everything they touched. Alarms sounded here, too, rallying for evacuation.

Turning back to Vala and Stefan, Francis said, "Go help the others escape the port, and get yourselves to safety while you're at it."

"What about you?" Vala asked.

"I need to go find Natasha."

She nodded. "Okay. Stay safe, Francis." She grabbed him in a tight hug.

"Yeah, stay safe," Stefan said. He clapped Francis again on the shoulder—damn, it hurt—and then he and his wife were away.

Francis turned and looked through the crowds of people. Somewhere out there was Mikhail, and if they were lucky, Natasha.

Gritting his teeth and wiping the blood from his eyebrow, Francis pushed into the crowd.

7

Fighting the masses was almost impossible. For every step Francis took forward, he only seemed to be bustled another to the side, another back. How he made any progress at all, he didn't know.

He grabbed at someone passing. "Have you seen—" But the man just looked at him with terror, then pushed his way out of Francis's grip and disappeared into the throng.

Francis cast terrified eyes in all directions. There were so many people! How could he find Natasha and Mikhail through all this?

Then he remembered the communicator. He'd snapped it onto

his wrist. Now he lifted it, cycled through the contacts, and found Mikhail's name.

Mikhail's answer was almost instant. "Miss Celeste?"

"It's Francis!"

"Francis? What are you doing with Ruby's communicator?"

"She gave it to me. Where are you?"

"Near the clock tower!"

Francis swivelled. There! Not too far from him, either.

"Stay there, I'm coming!"

"Hurry up! Everything is on fire!"

"I know!"

Francis shoved through and found himself back at the open central area's edge. Fewer people were here, and he sprinted alongside storefronts until he reached the clock tower—the tallest thing on *Cacophonous Harmonics*—and, beneath it, Mikhail. Mikhail nodded at Francis, and the two began to jog around the outside of the square.

"Have you seen her?" Francis asked.

"No. I've tried asking, but everyone's too distracted. But this place is small. There aren't too many places she can be."

Francis's eyes roved. Faces, dozens and dozens of them, but none the one he was searching for. "Are you sure she's even here?" he said desperately. "What if she was killed in the blast?"

"She wasn't."

"How—"

Francis didn't finish the sentence. Mikhail pushed ahead. There was a tiny little public garden outlined by bushes—and sprawled out in the remains of a plant much flatter than the others was the navigation leader's long, unmoving body.

8

Francis sprinted the last of the distance and skidded to a halt. Mikhail had already squatted beside Natasha, hands fussing.

"Is she—"

"She's alive," Mikhail said.

"How did she end up here?"

Mikhail shrugged. "Tossed this way in the blast? Either way, she's safe. Needs medical attention, but ..." He looked her over carefully. "No cuts, at least on this side. Maybe breaks ..." He trailed off and gave Francis an uneasy grin. "Can you tell I'm not a doctor?"

"We'll find one. Darrel, or someone on the port."

So Natasha was okay. Or seemed to be, anyway. And that was good.

"Listen, can you stay with her? Or get her to safety?" said Francis.

"I think so. Why?"

Francis looked back at the wreckage of the ship.

"There's something I need to do."

9

This time the struggle through the crowd was easier. Already people were filtering out of the SkyPort, making Francis's fight simpler. Still, it was only a diminished form of chaos, and it was not without effort that he crossed the concourse, asking people as he went if they'd seen a red-haired woman with a bandage about her waist. Very few answered, and of those that did, no one had seen her.

Which likely meant she was still on the ship.

When at last he reached it, he sprinted around the outside. There had to be an opening somewhere; no way could he climb two metres of shredded steel to enter through the hole he, Vala and Stefan had tumbled from. Surely there was an easier way.

There. The cavern that had, until a few days ago, been the porthole. It was sideways now, a great mouth-like doorway into darkness.

Darkness from which smoke poured.

Well, this was as good as it got. Clapping his arm over his

mouth, Francis jogged through the hole and back into the Pantheon.

As familiar as he'd become with its walkways, suddenly the Pantheon was strange. Tipped on its side, the corridors were misshapen and pocked with holes. Wood panelling had come off, exposing metal that was brown and frayed in the few places Francis had light enough to see by. Which wasn't often: only the occasional bulb remained aglow that Francis slowly crept toward, bowed low so as to avoid the smoke that hung to the ceiling.

"Ruby?" he called. The noise was muffled through his arm. Inhaling deeply, he removed it and shouted, "Ruby!"

No answer.

What if she had escaped the ship after all? What if it was empty now, and he was willingly walking deeper into its flaming bowels? It could collapse on him at any moment, or something might give and he'd be enveloped by choking smoke. He could die in here, looking for someone who had already left—

"Ruby!"

He hurtled forward. Splayed out in a heap was a body: shorter than him by an inch, a bandage around the middle, topped off with tangled crimson hair and a tricorne hat.

"Ruby! Are you okay?" He squatted, rolled her over. Probably weren't supposed to touch the injured, but damn it, they needed to get out of here. Now he'd removed his arm from his face, he could smell just how much smoke clogged the air. Every breath was harder than the last.

Ruby's eyes rolled back in her head. Francis shook her by the shoulders; no movement.

"*Ruby! Wake up, damn it!*"

He shook her again. This time a flicker, and then her eyes drifted slowly back into focus. She looked at Francis as though through a veil, and her eyebrows arced in confusion.

"Francis?" she heaved.

"Get up," he said, already pulling her to her feet. "Come on, we're getting you out of here."

"I told you—"

"I know what you told me," he said. "And we found Natasha. So I came back for you. Now use your legs, damn it, like you told me to when we boarded the Modicum. One foot, then another, got it?"

She obeyed: mercifully, she obeyed. They hobbled back the way Francis had come, breath hard under the smoke.

A misstep, and the floor beneath Francis's foot gave way. Smoke erupted from the hole and he wheeled backward. Fire roared underneath, glowing through the cleft.

"My ship," Ruby sobbed.

"Come on," said Francis. "We've got to go."

They skirted the newest wound, treading carefully. Like the Modicum had before, it held. Francis didn't know how, but he wasn't about to question their good luck.

A light shone ahead, blinding against the darkness. The exit.

"Come on," Francis coughed. "Almost there."

They took the last dozen metres as fast as Ruby could go, finally spilling out into the open. Racked by coughs, Francis wanted nothing more than to crash to the ground and breathe until his lungs were clean again. But he held firm and gripped Ruby as she clung to him for support, coughing feebly herself.

"Let me see," she whispered. "I want to see my ship."

"I don't think—"

"Please."

The woman staring at him now was broken. Soot dirtied her face, lines cut by tears. Blood still trickled from one corner of her lips, and now it really was black, dyed by the smoke.

"Let me see."

Francis obliged. Hobbling slowly, they turned. The Pantheon came into view—and Ruby howled.

"My ship! My—my ship!"

She fought to be free, but Francis held tighter. "Ruby—no—you can't—"

"*My ship!* It—it's ruined!"

"Ruby—"

"Let me go!" she begged. "Please—just let me—*my ship*! *What's happened to it?*"

Francis tugged. She was hysterical, fighting with all her might. Thank goodness for the wound in her side, because Francis might not have been able to hold her steady otherwise.

"Ruby, there's nothing we can do," he said. "Come on, we need to get out of here. This whole place is going to burn down, your ship included—and us, if we don't move."

The captain sobbed, pressed a bloodied hand to her face. She heaved with spasms as she bawled. But she stopped fighting, and Francis held her tight as she mourned the Pantheon's loss.

"Come on," he said.

"Okay," she finally conceded. "L-let's go."

Giving her ship one last look, Ruby allowed Francis to pivot her. They began to lurch toward the open end of the port; with it, the parking bay, and with that, perhaps, the promise of safety.

10

Rhod had docked. He didn't expect Celeste to have remained on her wrecked ship; she was probably somewhere on the port. And amidst the chaos, thinning out though it was as ships began to make their escape from *Cacophonous Harmonics*, he didn't think it would be a very easy task to find the woman.

But he knew how he *could* locate her.

Though many hundreds of miles out, Rhod kept good tabs on all his competitors. That was the way you controlled an empire and drove profits: by watching what everyone else was doing, and then doing a better job of it yourself. So he made sure he knew what every SkyPort sold, specialised in, as well as the comings and goings of the smaller businesses that sometimes set up residence in a rented spot.

Along with that, and not exactly necessary but of interest nonetheless, Rhod liked to keep track of the private aspects of each port too. Their staff facilities, warehouses, how their engineering team worked … Not for any reason, expressly. Just that it interested him.

And perhaps came in handy if he needed to send Imelda's men in to deal with a competitor.

So he knew, as he barrelled a path across *Cacophonous Harmonics*, that the SkyPort had an office to the rear helmed by a man named Keith Bracken. And he also knew that this office was used to review the port's many camera feeds; cameras which should still be functional. Mostly.

Cameras he could use to find Celeste.

Rhod thundered into the office, kicking the door off its hinges. Keith jerked in his direction. He was a skinny man, in the middle of a phone call—probably desperately trying to figure out what the hell had happened in the past ten minutes. He gave Rhod a terrified look—and then Rhod withdrew his pistol and pulled the trigger, wiping the look off his face.

Rhod strode around the desk. Televisions painted the wall in two rows of four. Three displays were replaced by static. The others showed views of the port, almost all of which were painted yellow with flame. A couple showed the open area in the centre of the port, which was almost clear, while another was half-focussed on the wreckage of the Pantheon. Rhod scrutinised this most closely, but nothing exited except smoke.

So Celeste had left. The question now was, where was she?

He kicked Keith's body to one side, ignoring the shrill voice that squawked away on the other end of the phone—it would go silent in a moment; always did—and sat in the dead man's seat. Then he stared at screens, searching.

It didn't take long.

There: Celeste, with that stupid pirate hat on her head, clutching a man who looked oddly familiar. Rhod leaned forward. Was that the deckhand she'd stolen?

It *was*!

Well, wasn't *that* rosy.

Rhod smiled. He reached for the microphone that directed *Cacophonous Harmonics's* intercom system, licked his lips, and pressed the transmit button.

"Good afternoon, patrons of *Cacophonous Harmonics*. I'd like to apologise for blowing a hole in the port just now; rest assured I intended no harm to come to the majority of you at this point of commerce.

"But you, Ruby Celeste," he continued. "I very much intend for harm to come to you. And it will; I can see that you're injured." The woman on the screen stopped, and Rhod smirked as two heads searched for the source of the transmission. "That's right, Celeste. I can see you, and your little friend.

"I'm coming for you. And do you know what I'm going to do when I get there? I'm going to kill you. And maybe I'll kill *him,* too.

"Oh, and by the way," he added offhandedly. "I wouldn't run. I'll only make it slower if you do."

Ending the announcement, Rhod gave a final look at Celeste's location, then reached down and lifted up one trouser leg. There, in a leather pouch wrapped around a meaty ankle, was his dagger. He drew it out, looked over its sleek, glinting surface with a malevolent smile, and then marched around the desk and from the office.

11

For a long second, Ruby and Francis stood stock still, neither sure what to do. Then Rhod's final words clanged back to Francis, and he pulled at Ruby once more.

"Come on. We're almost there. If we move—"

"We don't have time," Ruby said.

"If we're quick—"

"No!" Ruby cried. Her eyes were panicked orbs of white. "There's no time! I can't move fast enough. But—but you can!" She tried to extract herself from Francis's grip, but he held on.

"Francis, let go! You can get to safety!"

"I can save you—"

"*Francis, please!*" she shouted desperately. Wet lines streaked her face. "It's me he wants, not you! If you hide—look, over here!" She pulled, somehow dragging him around in a half-circle and across to the nearest storefront. "Down here, in this little nook by the door." She unwound her arms; Francis fought to grab her, but somehow she was too quick. "Just hide here, okay?"

"Ruby—"

"*Please*, Francis." Just as they had in the Pantheon's control centre, her eyes begged. "Please, just stay here until he's gone. It's me he wants. You—you can survive. You can live."

"But—"

Ruby sniffed. Swiped sooty tears from her face. She drew in a deep breath. "You're part of my crew now. That's an order, Francis. Hide. Be safe. *Live*."

How much time had passed since Rhod's announcement? Where had he even delivered it from? Francis didn't know, and every second longer they waited …

"Okay," he whispered at last. He crouched in the alcove. Two potted plants were stood to either side, and he positioned behind the leftmost one as best he could. Ruby pushed his shoulders to shrink him further. "That's the best I can do," he said.

Ruby nodded. "Okay."

"Please be—"

But Francis didn't get to finish, because Ruby was gone.

12

One hand clutched against her bandaged side, Ruby hobbled toward the edge of the SkyPort. It was a dozen metres away, no more. Maybe Francis was right: maybe they could have made it. But if they didn't, that would have meant Francis was with her when she failed, and she didn't want to endanger his life any more. She'd done that enough.

Before she was even half the distance, a voice called out from behind her, "Celeste!"

She turned. Thundering forward, a victorious grin plastered across his face, was Rhod Stein. More than six feet tall, two hundred and fifty pounds of muscle and fat: a hulking behemoth, bearing down on her.

So. This was it. The end.

13

"Good afternoon, Mr Stein," Ruby started. The words didn't quite finish leaving her mouth: Rhod crossed the last distance between them and slapped her hard across the face. Her head jerked; blood sprayed.

"Good afternoon *nothing*," he barked. He gripped her face and pressed the steel dagger to her neck. The point dug in. She quivered, and a trickle of blood dribbled down. "I've waited for this moment for a long time, Celeste."

Ruby's breath shuddered. "Do it slow," she grunted. "I promise I won't cry."

"Hah! Talking it up," Rhod growled. He pressed his face close in to Ruby's. "Maybe I *should* make it slow, just to see."

"Just don't chicken out halfway. I imagine this is the first time you've done the dirty work yourself."

"You think wrong."

"With a knife?" Ruby grimaced—the best smile she could pull. "I'm impressed. Most folk use guns. Then again, that knife's awful sharp. Perhaps there's a first time for everything."

Rhod glared. He pushed the knife in harder; Ruby twitched beneath him, and the rivulet of crimson thickened. "You know nothing."

"I know I blew a hole in your SkyPort and made off with the man you kidnapped to try to sell to me. You won't find him, by the way," she added. When she spoke, her teeth were red, and blood trickled over the edges of her lips. "I told him to escape. No sense both of us dying. He's probably gone already."

"Doesn't matter. You're the only one I want." Rhod grinned. "And now I have you."

"Took you four men and almost two weeks of searching. The mighty Rhod Stein. Bested by a girl." Ruby smirked. "Shameful."

The blood boiled in Rhod's cheeks. "Don't you dare—"

"Too late."

They stared at each other for a second, Rhod's face a contorted mask of utter loathing, Ruby's face squeezed under his grip but smug nonetheless—*so damn smug*.

And right then, Rhod knew he was going to make this quick.

"*Fuck you!*"

He released the woman, swung the dagger up in the air, and brought it down.

14

This was Ruby's one chance. She wanted to survive this, of course she did, unlikely though the odds were. And she *would* fight.

So as Rhod swung, Ruby used all the strength she had left in her body to do the thing she was best at: she drew her sword with a glorious *shick*, arcing it up and in front of her body—

Metal clanged on metal as dagger and sword hit.

The dagger flew backward, skittering out of Rhod's grasp and out of sight.

The sword also flew from Ruby's hands.

"No!" she yelled.

But too late—it pirouetted to the edge of the SkyPort, bounced precariously at the precipice, and then disappeared.

"My sword—"

Rhod's hands found her neck.

Her eyes bulged. She turned to look into his blazing face, tried to gasp for air, and couldn't.

"Move," Rhod instructed.

She didn't.

"*Move*," he repeated. "To the edge. *Now*."

She tried to choke out a 'no', but nothing came.

Rhod growled, "Then I'll do it."

And he did.

15

From his vantage point, Francis watched in terror. His view was half obscured by leathery leaves, but he witnessed enough: saw Rhod approaching Ruby; saw their exchange as he pressed the dagger into her neck; saw Rhod swing it at her, and saw Ruby's defense, before both sword and dagger flew in opposite directions. Where the sword went, he wasn't sure—that was just out of view—but the dagger; he could see that. It had come to a stop barely a metre from him. Francis had frozen, terrified that Rhod would come for it to finish the job.

But he hadn't. Instead he'd gripped Ruby by the neck, and was now—*walking her to the edge of the SkyPort!*

Francis peered out. Rhod's back was to him; Ruby, dwarfed, was behind, out of view. They were just steps from the edge now.

Was he going to make her step off? Just like that? Or would he throttle her, squeeze until she was almost gone, and then throw her over so she had the barest wits about her as she plummeted to her death?

He's killing her. You've got to do something.

But what? Ruby had summed it up perfectly the first time they met: Francis weighed all of one-fifty soaking wet. What could he do?

She's going to die, and you're the only one that can help. You've got to do something!

He looked around desperately. But what could he do up against the giant man?

And then his eyes landed on it: the dagger.

16

They were at the edge of the port. One step and they would be right at the terminus, and an inch more and they would be over.

Ruby would be over. Because she couldn't fight Rhod. Her whole body screamed, the wound in her side most of all. It had taken all the energy she had to stop him from stabbing her, and for what? So he could toss her overboard instead.

"No one gets one over on Rhod Stein," he breathed. "*No one.* Not you, not anyone else. Sometimes people think they do, but they always pay the price. *Always*. And now it's your turn, Celeste. You've evaded me for a long time, been a real thorn in my side. But not anymore."

His grip tightened, harder, harder. Ruby tried to gasp, tried to breathe, but he was too powerful. Her eyes bulged; her cheeks reddened as blood rushed to her face.

Her lungs first groaned, then screamed in desperation. She tried to suck, to take even the tiniest gasp of air—but nothing would come.

All she could do was wait to die, knowing the last thing she ever saw would be Rhod Stein's great, ugly, leering face. And that horrible grin, knowing that he had, at last, won.

17

"You've evaded me for a long time, been a real thorn in my side. But not anymore."

Francis snuck from his cover. He was sure Rhod would turn, see him. His hands shook. But Rhod didn't move, and Francis slid the dagger into his grip carefully, weighing it in his hand.

He stared at the behemoth's back. His heart thrummed.

I can't, part of him whispered.

But another said, *You have to!*

He was still, frozen.

And then: *Go! Now!*

Gripping the dagger tight, Francis swallowed hard. He straightened, prayed to whatever god might be out there that he could do this.

And then, with a last deep breath, he sprang.

18

Francis hurtled forward, crossing the distance in four long strides. He let out a battle cry as he leapt, drew the dagger up—

Rhod, at the sound of the footsteps, started to turn—

And then the dagger plunged into his neck.

19

Rhod roared. He released Ruby, pushed her away hard, and clawed at his neck. But he had twisted, so Ruby didn't go overboard; instead she landed in a heap to his side, drawing in a great heaving gasp of breath. And Rhod didn't manage to stay still, because whoever had embedded this knife into his neck—his *own* knife, he was sure of it—had collided with him just hard enough to transfer a little bit of momentum, and—

Rhod's footing went. He struggled to regain it, but his body continued forward and his feet tried to keep up. One, then the other—

Except that other foot hit the very edge of the SkyPort, half on, half off. He teetered, bellowed—

And with one final cry, Rhod Stein tumbled out of sight.

20

Ruby didn't know how long she lay there, but someone was crouched next to her, talking: words she didn't quite understand. It was Francis, a dim part of her finally realised; Francis again, Francis who'd saved her life three times now, and the first of those after she'd directly accused him of feeding information to Stein and leading attackers to her.

She blinked and tried to focus. The world rippled, and black streaked the air; smoke from the growing flames. With another sharp inhale—it hurt so much, but felt so good—she brought Francis into focus. He was pale.

"What happened?" she wheezed.

"I killed him," Francis said. "I—at least, I think. He—he fell over the side. He's not going to bother us anymore." He let out a very short nervous laugh, then fell silent. In Ruby's vision, he split into two. She tried her best to reconcile them, but the copies of Francis refused to merge. "We need to get you out of here. I think you've ripped your stitches."

Ruby nodded. The welts on her neck screamed. "I can't walk."

"I—I could carry you?"

"No, you couldn't."

Francis bit his lip. "I think you're right."

The world slipped out of view a little bit. Ruby breathed deep and concentrated hard on bringing it back. It seemed just a little darker at the edges, but it held. For now.

"Trove," she said. "Call Trove."

Francis nodded. He lifted the communicator, cycled through, and then radioed for Trove. Just a moment later, Trove's voice came through: "Miss Celeste? Are you all right?"

"It's Francis. I've got Ruby here."

"Is she okay? We heard the announcement, and—"

"I'm fine, Trove," said Ruby. Francis extended the communicator toward her. "We're okay. Francis saved me." Her eyes met his, just for an instant. "How is everyone else?"

"All accounted for," Trove answered. "We're still in the parking bay. Were waiting for you, actually."

"I can't—" Ruby's voice trailed off. She slumped backward. Francis gripped her shoulder; she snaked up a weak hand and held him.

"She can't walk," Francis said. "And I can't lift her. Can you pick us up?"

"Absolutely. Where are you?"

"Erm—at the edge of the SkyPort. You'll see us."

"On it. Be there in a moment."

Francis switched the communicator off. He stooped beside Ruby. Her eyes were closed, her breathing laboured. Beneath her free hand, her bandages were stained crimson.

"Sit tight, Ruby," he muttered. "We'll be out of here soon."

Harbinger

(Epilogue)

1

Dear Mum and Dad;

I don't know if you ever received my letter. And I don't know if you'll receive this one. But I sincerely hope you do; both of them, ideally, but if not then just this one will suffice.

I've thought long and hard over this, and decided that you can disregard everything I said before. When I said it was dangerous up here—well, okay, yes, that is true. It is dangerous. But I'm in safe hands.

I won't get too bogged down in specifics. Not yet, anyway; I still need some time to wrap my head around everything. But just know that your son is doing okay.

I hope to see you again soon.

Your loving son;

Francis Paige.

Francis re-read the letter. It was brief, but would do. For now the most important thing was simply keeping his parents informed—if they received this short note. They might not, and Francis might never know either way. But he had to believe.

He re-checked the address on the inside and outside, then folded it tight.

"Ready?" Natasha asked.

He glanced up at her. She stood in the door to the Harbinger's library; larger than the Pantheon's, and with more books too. For all the bruises and broken bones, she was healing up nicely.

"Yep. Let's go."

They walked through the ship side by side. It was strange, getting used to new corridors. The layout was entirely different to the Pantheon's. And despite the short time Francis had been on that ill-fated ship, its interior had become so ingrained he was sure it would be months before he forgot it and adapted to the Harbinger's sleeker, newer confines.

Instead of a porthole, a minute third deck open to the sunlight was perched atop the ship, with a regular door leading topside. Francis passed the usual trio of workhands assisting Vala and Stefan filling the new glass-topped room with plants, and gave a little hello as he passed.

Outside, the sky was tinted purple, and entirely unobstructed. No towering fins above the Harbinger: these fanned out in smaller arrangements along the ship's side and underbelly instead.

Cacophonous Harmonics had been well-insured. And though it was down to Rhod Stein that the Pantheon had been felled, along with the SkyPort, Ruby had somehow wrangled this ship out of the ether. Compensation, apparently. Francis wasn't sure he quite believed it, but he didn't feel like arguing. He'd lost two homes these past six weeks, and was itching to get back into another one.

Francis and Natasha wandered to Harbinger's railing. In the weeks it had been since the Pantheon crash-landed, they had been shuttled about between SkyPort and SkyPort, city and city. Finally they were back above land; perfect timing, given Francis had just managed to finish this letter after weeks of trying.

Extending his hand, Francis silently wished his note luck, and dropped it.

"Do you think they'll get it?" Natasha asked.

"I hope so."

For a while they were silent. Then footsteps sounded on the deck behind, and both turned.

Ruby approached. Her lip was mended, as was her side, though Francis suspected she still fell under Darrel's near-constant surveillance. She smiled, and said, "Evening. Mind if I speak with Mr Paige alone?"

Natasha nodded. "See you shortly, Francis."

She loped off. Francis watched her go, and then nodded to Ruby. "Evening."

"Evening," Ruby said.

They were quiet for an awkward moment. Then Ruby joined Francis at the railing, held, and looked out into the approaching dusk.

"I've been meaning to thank you," she said. "And apologise."

"Oh?"

"I was so sure you were the cause of everything, when really ... it was me. I'm sorry for that." She looked down, then turned to Francis. "I accused you of being a spy. Working for him. And then you saved me. Not once, but three times." She looked perplexed. "Why?"

"When I arrived here, you said that this ship was like a family. I fought it at first, because I was desperate to go home—and I hated you, because I thought you'd taken the only avenue back from me." Francis glanced at her sidelong and pulled a wan smile. "That's something *I'm* sorry for." Looking back out over land, he continued, "But then I began to slot into your crew—that family— and realised how wonderful everyone is. And Rhod was sending those people after us—after *you*. And that made me realise just how much of a bad person he is.

"At first ... for a long time, really ... I thought you'd kidnapped me," Francis said slowly. "But you didn't: you rescued me. And even if you were suspicious, I never forgot that. You rescued me from him. So I did the same." He shrugged. "I've never been very eloquent. If that was a mess to understand ..."

"It wasn't." Ruby smiled. "Thank you, Francis. For saving me."

They were quiet for a little longer. The sky darkened, slowly, and the moon began to rise. Before long it would be the only light.

"I expect you're curious what I'm doing here," Ruby said.

"That wasn't it?"

"Well, not entirely. I brought *this*."

She produced a leatherbound book.

"The diary," said Francis. "From the Modicum."

"That's right." Ruby flicked through its pages. "I was so convinced that what it said was true."

"So are we still looking for it?" Francis asked. "The Ghost Armada."

The captain shook her head.

"Why?"

"Because over the past couple of weeks, while I recovered, I came to understand a few things." Ruby sighed. "This is complicated, and I'm not very precise with words either, but I'll do my best.

"In the wake of Benjamin's untimely demise, I've been doing some research. And after a while, I stumbled upon knowledge of a *parasite*. Some call it Malaise, others called it Démence; the name varies, but its effects are the same, and rather recognisable."

"What does it do?"

"Initially, it infects a Volum," Ruby said matter-of-factly. "It's starts slow-growing, but then breeds exponentially, causing all manner of effects. Loss of lift ... corrodes metal ... causes insanity in a ship's crew ..."

"The Modicum."

"That's right. We thought it was rusted—"

"Just like we thought the rust in the Pantheon was caused by the condenser malfunctioning," said Francis. "But it was a parasite?"

"Correct. A parasite that infected our Volum—and then poor Ben, given the amount of time he spent with it. I daresay if we'd survived much longer the rest of us might have turned too.

"The more I read, the more I realised. This diary—it's exactly what everyone thought: the diary of a madman. Filled with deranged writings and lunatic ideas—ideas about ethereal ships. A Ghost Armada." Ruby pulled a sad smile. "And that's why I've come: to do this."

She extended the diary over the Harbinger's edge, and let it drop. Francis tracked it as it fell, tumbling through the dark until he could see it no more.

"And now, Francis, I want to make you a promise." Turning, Ruby looked at him squarely. "I don't know how, nor if it will happen. But if ever an opportunity arises, I *will* get you home."

Elation swelled in Francis's chest. He nodded. "Thank you."

"I rather think it's you *I* should be thanking."

Momentary quiet. Then Ruby nodded curtly and said, "Well. I'd best be off. I believe dinner will be served shortly."

She turned and trekked away.

"Ruby?"

She paused.

Francis hesitated. "How old are you?"

"What?"

"Natasha said the Pantheon was older than her, and definitely older than you. But she's about my age, I thought. So …"

"I see. And how old are you, Francis?"

"Twenty-four."

"Well. Okay then."

She turned again, and Francis called, "You didn't answer."

Ruby looked at him over her shoulder. "I know. A lady never tells her age." Then, setting off along the deck once more, she said, "See you later, Francis."

2

Francis frowned and turned back out to look over the edge of the ship, marvelling at how far he'd come. Just weeks ago he hadn't been able to do this, and now …

He paused. Up ahead something glinted in the dark; something shadowy, silhouetted by the moon. He squinted. It had looked like … but …

No. It couldn't have been.

Could it?

Shaking the image from his mind, Francis turned and headed back into the ship. He was hungry and seeing things. Because there was no way he had seen, just for an instant, a mass of ships against the glowing white face of the moon before they blinked out of sight.

After all, they had been just the words of a madman. There was no Ghost Armada. Certainly not.

Read Ruby's next adventure now!

RUBY CELESTE
AND THE DIRE KRAKEN

Captained by Morris Flute, the two-man trade ship Exceptional Luck has lived up to its name—at least until coming under attack in a sprawling floating rainforest. In his last moments, Flute desperately fights to drop a beacon—and then something streaks from the abyss and his world turns black.

Meanwhile, on the Harbinger, Ruby Celeste's crew are enjoying the height of summer. All except for Francis, who finds himself victimised by the awkward pursuit of Brie Channing, one of the ship's night-shift technicians. It is her he thinks has woken him one morning; but instead he finds a drone affixed to his window, issuing a brief distress call.

The drone leads to an abandoned weather station and its sole remaining inhabitant, Tesla Wong, who tells of the Exceptional Luck's beacon. Allured by the promise of rare gemstones, Ruby decides to investigate. Now she and her crew press forward in search of the downed trade ship and its lost cargo. But the Exceptional Luck's last details were scant, and neither Ruby nor her crew know they are flying straight into danger, destined for conflict with a terrifying beast: the dire kraken.

Afterword

Thank you so much for taking the time to read *Ruby Celeste and the Ghost Armada*. It's incredible to me that this book is finished—not least because its first seeds began to grow in my mind in early 2010. Three full years, and four attempts, it has taken to write this story—and I could not be happier with how it has turned out.

I hope you've enjoyed the book. If you could take the time to write a review, I would sincerely appreciate it. Even if you hated it; reviews communicate feedback not only to other readers, but also to me as I move forward with the series.

If you're looking for more information on me or the Ruby Celeste universe, be sure to take a visit to Regarding THE HIVE at www.regardingthehive.co.uk. The website holds a dedicated section for Ruby Celeste with Wiki-esque pages on various aspects of the world you've seen so far, including brand new information you won't see in the books. So whether you hunger for pointless trivia, or want to dig further into the Rubyverse, be sure to give it a look!

Finally, I love to hear from readers! If you want to get in touch, find me on Twitter @nj_ambrose, or send me an email at nicholas@regardingthehive.co.uk.

Nicholas J. Ambrose

CPSIA information can be obtained at www.ICGtesting.com
Printed in the USA
LVOW10s1321050416

482252LV00025B/343/P